HIGHLAND STORM

GUARDIANS OF SCOTLAND BOOK 2

VICTORIA ZAK

Sign up for Victoria Zak's newsletter on her website to receive a free ebook copy of her
Guardians of Scotland novella
Highland Destiny

You'll also find additional special offers, bonus content and info on new releases.

www.victoriazakromance.com
victoria@victoriazakromance.com

facebook.com/VictoriaZakAuthor

bookbub.com/authors/victoria-zak

instagram.com/victoriazakromance

twitter.com/VictoriaZak2

Highland Storm, Guardians of Scotland Book 2
Victoria Zak
Copyright 2014 by Victoria Zak

All rights reserved. Except as permitted under the U.S. Copyright Act 1976, no part of this publication may be reproduced, distributed, or transmitted in any form or by any means, or stored in a database or retrieval system without prior written permission of the author and publisher.

All characters, events, and locations in this book are fictitious. Any similarity to real persons, dead or living, is coincidental and not intended by the author.

Cover Design by JAB Designs

Editing by Violetta Rand

❦ Created with Vellum

1

Cold sweat streamed down Conall Hamilton's face and his heartbeat quickened as he sat up in bed, catching his breath. Ever since he'd dared to dream of a solitary life and settling down with a woman, haunting images of his past plagued his nights. Visions of his beautiful wife and son running into his arms should have been his last memory of his family, but Conall wasn't granted that pleasure. Instead, his last memory was of Ann and wee Thomas brutally murdered outside their village by a band of rogue Vikings.

Yet tonight's dream had been different. There had been no charred bodies, no screams, and no dirty little feet poking out from under the white sheet that covered his son's lifeless body. Indeed, this dream was different, it had come with a message.

Conall shut his eyes tight, trying to erase the nightmare from his mind. He shoved his hands through his sweaty hair and cursed. "Holy hell!" Ann was there; he had felt her.

He recalled her warm gentle hands caressing his chest, slowly making their way under the covers, where he grew aroused from the sweet torture. His hands found their way up her long legs straddling his hips. *By the saints, they are soft.*

The fresh smell of rain wisped past his nose, awakening all of his senses. Silky strands of long hair tickled his cheek and her voice warmed his heart like a summer's breeze. "Wake up, me darling."

This had to be a dream, yet the body spanning him felt so real. And her scent... God, her scent. Even though centuries had passed, that scent never did. Conall rubbed his hands up and down her soft thighs and opened his eyes. "Nay, 'tis a dream."? In disbelief, he ran his hands through her golden locks. "Ann."

"Aye, me darling," she said sweetly. His wife felt of flesh and blood; her flawless, white skin shimmered with a glow as he trailed his hands down her shoulders and cupped her breasts. "If this be a dream, I do no' want to wake," he whispered.

Ann bent down and kissed his lips. Her lips were just as he remembered, full, soft and made for passionate kisses. Whispering in between kisses, Conall said, "I've missed ye, *mo chridhe*."

The beautiful woman sat up and smiled brightly down at her husband. "'Tis time, Conall."

"For what?" He didn't want to waste time with useless chatter. He knew what he wanted to do. It was what he had longed to do since the day she was unfairly and brutally taken away from him. Claim her one last time.

Conall pulled Ann down on top of him but was halted. "Nay, Conall, ye must listen to me. 'Tis time to move on and allow yourself to love again."

Another vision flashed through him. He was on bended knees, gathering up his family's ashes, preparing for his pilgrimage to the holy land. Ann and Thomas, his wee Thomas, needed a proper burial away from the ruin of their home and the evil of men. He owed it to them. They deserved peace and their souls needed to be put to rest properly.

Never allowing himself forgiveness for failing to protect his family, he roamed the earth. He was a shell of a man. With every step he took he mourned his family. Being immortal, Dragonkine warriors gave part of their immortality to their wives. They had eternity to be together. So he had thought.

As he watched her smiling down over him, he remembered that long, daunting journey. It seemed as if it had happened only yesterday, not centuries ago. Even being a dragon, the road to the holy place was dangerous. It left many travelers meeting their maker sooner than they expected. Whether it was inner peace, to be forgiven for crimes, or seeking a cure for illness, the voyagers endured the crusade, seeking spiritual enlightenment.

One night, on his way to the holy land, Conall had sought refuge at a nearby village tavern where he was greeted by an unruly group of local folk. Desperate to rob Conall of everything, the men began to beat him. After the first blow, the warrior discovered he could actually feel again. Blow by blow, his body absorbed each pounding fist as he stood stoic. He believed that this was his punishment for failing his wife.

Bloodied and bruised, Conall stood in the middle of the dark, stale tavern with his body giving up when a man from out of the shadows came to his rescue. Conall had been one blow away from being knocked on his arse when his rescuer grabbed the bastard's fist before it connected with his face. Bones shattered in the rogue's hand as he screamed out in pain. The rest of the thieves scattered with one look at Conall's rescuer.

The man from the shadows looked Conall up and down and then shook his head in disgust. "I know who you are, lad. Come with me and you will find what you seek."

Conall wiped the blood from his lips. "Ye know nothing, auld man," he bit back. He turned to the serving wench who was standing nearby. "Ale."

The stranger grinned and took the seat next to Conall. "Lad, you seek the holy land, this I know." He motioned for the wench to fill his cup, too. "For what reason, 'tis for you to keep. I'm only offering you our protection."

Conall laughed. Mortal men offering him, a Dragonkine, protection. This was ludicrous. He housed a dragon deep inside of him, for God's sake. He was far more dangerous and capable of taking care of his own affairs. "Och, if ye know who I be, ye would know that I dinnae need yer protection."

"Aye, spoken like a true Highlander." The man took a long pull of his freshly poured ale.

The man who came from the shadows was beginning to irritate him. "Who are ye?"

"Hugues de Payens." He took another long swallow of ale. "I and my brethren," he motioned over to a corner of the room, "offer you our protection in reaching the holy land. We are the Knights Templar."

It was like a cold hand reaching up and slapping him right upside the head. He had heard about the Templars and how they helped folks. They were brave knight-warriors, a wealthy military religious order.

Although he was impressed by the mere appearance of the man, something was unsettling. How did Hugues know who he was?

As if the man had read his thoughts, he began to explain. "It's been written in the scrolls that a Dragonkine warrior would cross our path and become the ninth Templar. Conall, my friend, this is your next journey in life. Join us."

Skeptical, Conall sat silent for a while. True, he needed to fulfill his quest, yet could he trust these men? Without a doubt, with their help, his journey wouldn't be as daunting compared to going alone. His wife and son needed to be laid to rest, and for that reason alone, he would join the Templars.

Conall rubbed the tension from his neck. "Aye, I'll join ye, but as soon as me quest is complete, I'm on me own. Understood?"

The Templar rubbed his hands over his white-robed thighs and grinned. "Aye." As the image of his wife came back into view, he recalled how much he'd changed. Before Ann, he'd been alone and angry, stranded in a human world without his Kine. King MacAlpin, king of the Scots, had slaughtered his people and destroyed his kingdom. He'd lost so much that he was positive the elders had damned him for eternity.

Even though the king of Scots had left behind seven Dragonkine warriors to serve him, they had parted ways, broken and angry. The pain and loss was unbearable, which had led Conall down his path of destruction. He battled with rage and he didn't care what side he fought on as long as he was killing humans.

But Ann had changed everything. She'd brought light to his darkness. She was the air he breathed.

Aye, there had been a time when life had been good. Alas, it had been no more than a blink of an eye.

After his wife and son's death, he didn't want to slip back into the dark past. He had to move on. In honor of his late wife, for he knew Ann would be proud of him, he joined the Templars and fought for the greater good.

But all good things come to an end for a damned dragon.

Life had been good in France, until The Templars had become an economic threat to many kings. Conall had made it out of France just before the men he fought with were imprisoned for alleged crimes ranging from devil worship to homosexuality. The allegations burned Conall's soul. These men were honest and courageous, and he loathed the fact that he couldn't rescue them. One man, who had to keep his dragon secret, standing against the country of France, well, the odds were not in his favor. He'd had to flee to Scotland to avoid the same fate as his brethren.

Ann interrupted his inner musings. "Conall, ye have been forgiven a long time ago. Ye need to find love again and become whole. Yer dragon needs peace, me love."

Conall wished it was that easy to forgive himself but he couldn't. No matter how many times he'd tried to overcome the unbearable pain of losing his wife and son and the men who'd showed him a better life, he would never allow himself happiness, nor put another loved one in harm's way as long as he lived. Which, for an immortal, would be a very long time.

His beautiful wife took his head in her hands and looked into his eyes. "Do ye think it's fair to the red-headed lass ye've been courting? Ye must do the right thing and make an honest woman of her."

He hadn't quite thought about it like that. Keeping his and Effie's passion-filled jaunts a secret was the only way he knew to keep her safe and protect her from his enemies. Not once had he thought of how Effie might feel.

"I must go. Please heed me words and do the honorable thing, marry that lass."

When Conall looked back, her ghostly form was beginning to

fade. Desperately, he tried to hold onto her, but his hands passed right through her disappearing body. "Tell Thomas that his da loves him verra much." A tear slid from his eye as he saw Ann smile right before she crumbled into smoldering ash and vanished into the air like smoke.

Now the warrior sat alone in his bedchamber, dazed and confused. The message had been firm. Marry Effie or let her go. He enjoyed the lass thoroughly. His dragon craved her relentlessly. But loving her could very well be the death of him.

Sitting up, Conall ran his hands through his hair and exhaled in frustration. Mayhap after a warm bath and with food in his belly he would be able to make the right decision.

After spending too much time in the bath, Conall climbed out of the tub, dried himself off, donned his kilt, tunic, and laced his boots. He grabbed his jerkin before he left his bedchamber. Not being able to commit one way or the other to Effie, frustration began to sour his mood. The more he thought about breaking her heart, the more he cursed himself for being a bastard.

Quickly, Conall descended the stairs leading into the great hall, slipping on his jerkin. Winter was upon them and it had been a bitter one. Being a storm dragon, Conall's powers came in handy. He'd cloaked Black Stone on the Hill and its surrounding village by redirecting the worst of the weather away from them, yet the cold still bit back frigidly. James, Laird of Angus and the Dragonkine commander, was quite thankful for his best friend's special abilities, for his wife, Abigale, was with child and working in the village as the clan's surgeon.

As he entered the great hall, empty trenchers were scattered about the tables indicating he'd missed the morning meal. Indeed, he'd pondered his situation with Effie for too long. It was time he found her and put an end to this torture. The sooner it was over, he could move on and concentrate on business. James had informed him that there was trouble brewing.

Clan Lockhart, a strong supporter of Robert the Bruce and allies of Clan Douglas, had missing cattle and their border was being breached by another neighboring clan. Conall and a few men were to leave on the morrow to investigate before a feud broke out. *Holy hell! Why can't there be peace for just one day?*

Chatter from the kitchen brought Conall's attention back to Effie. She had to be in there with Alice and Abigale, he thought. The three women were inseparable. Ever since Abigale had arrived at Black Stone on the Hill, the lassies had become close, forming a sisterly bond. Effie had told him numerous times that she'd finally got the sister she'd always wanted, and that Alice reminded her of her ma.

Sweat beaded across his forehead and his heart raced as he thought about how he was going to make it to that kitchen. As soon as she saw him, she would know what was going on. Effie could read him like a book. Not to mention, Alice and Abigale would have a few sharp words, scolding him for the bastard he was.

Conall began to pace, then finally he cursed himself a coward and started to approach the kitchen. As he crossed the threshold, Abigale greeted him. "Good morn, Conall."

"Good morn, ladies." He bowed his head.

"Someone missed the morning meal." Alice smiled and winked at Abigale as she chopped carrots.

"Aye, I do believe ye're right. Do ye suppose we have extra food for our belated guest?" Abigale said.

"Nay, Lennox and Mahboon cleaned up after the men left, but I'm sure an oatcake or two are left. Though probably stale by now."

Conall grinned in amusement as he leaned his shoulder against the wall. His tension eased as he realized he wouldn't be confronting Effie, at least not yet. He folded his arms across his chest. Abigale and Alice were relentless with their teasing. It was frowned upon to miss the morning meal. It was an act of rudeness, as Alice would say.

Alice placed her knife down and walked toward a counter where a steaming trencher of porridge sat. She grabbed the provisions and walked toward Conall. "Here." Alice sat the bowl down on a small table used for chopping in the center of the kitchen. "Grab a chair and dinnae be late again," she scolded.

"Aye, please accept me most humble apology." Conall grabbed a chair and brought it over to the table. He sat down to eat. "Hmm, Alice. 'Tis good," he said with his mouth full.

Alice shook her head and began chopping again.

"James and Rory are on top of the battlements teaching Neven archery. Will ye be joining them?" Abigale asked.

Neven? Archery? Now that was a dangerous combination. The lad, God bless his soul, had a nervous tick. Seeing his mum murdered had left the lad a bit on the jumpy side.

"Nay," Conall wiped his mouth, "I was wondering where Effie may be."

"Oh, she's down in the bailey fetching the lock and key the smith made for Alice," Abigale said.

Alice pointed her knife at Conall. "Aye, that should keep the wee bugger out of me oatcakes."

Neven was also well known for sneaking into the kitchen and stealing Alice's special oatcakes. The only reason Alice didn't bend the lad over her knee and swat his bum was because Laird James loved him like a son. Neven admired James, and the young lad couldn't have had a better role model.

Conall stopped mid-chew. "Effie went to see the smith? Alone?"

"Aye," Abigale confirmed.

'Twas not good. He began to panic. The lasses swooned over the smith, for he was known for his good looks, and charm. There was a rumor the man was well-endowed. Not that Conall was jealous. For Christ's sake, he was a dragon, but when it came to Effie, he didn't trust the blacksmith and his sly antics.

Conall shot up, causing the chair to slide and smash against the stone wall. "Excuse me. I must go."

Walking out of the door leading to the bailey, he pulled his cloak up around his neck as he passed Alice's herb garden, now withered, touched by the bite of winter. He made his way to the smithy.

Conall didn't have to go far, for the shop was close. Besides the smith's reputation with lasses, he was one hell of a craftsman when it came to armor; he could forge the finest weapons and the strongest swords. James had declared him the smith of the Dragonkine and gave him a forge close to the castle.

Conall rounded the corner and his heart dropped. Effie was entering the blacksmith's shop.

2

Effie Douglas, at least that was who she had been for the past five years, walked toward the bailey swinging her wicker basket back and forth, stopping every so often to search the merchant carts. Figs and grapes weren't what she sought, nor would she find the magical answer lying in a cart. She knew exactly what she wanted. She yearned for something more in life. As of late, Effie desired marriage. Tired of being her lover's secret, twas time to make changes in her life.

"A secret," she huffed. She was worth more.

She had left her clan and her older brother's brutality behind five years ago. It had taken that long to build herself up again. Tavish Maxwell was the devil incarnate. His verbal abuse as bad as his physical abuse. Calling her a worthless whore, he beat her into submission, and Effie had no choice but to submit.

Tavish made her do unspeakable things for his gain. Whoring her out to strangers. Fortunately for him, he had walked in on situation which had left Effie forever obeying his every word.

Effie often thought about: What if Tavish hadn't been spying on her that dreadful day? What if he hadn't seen her making love to the young man she had thought to marry? What if she'd had the courage to stand up for herself and tell her father? Nay, the look of disappointment on her father's face would ruin her. Effie made sure no one would find out about that day. She did what she had to do to keep her good reputation clean in her father's eyes, even if it tarnished her from the inside.

Effie came to an abrupt stop as she realized she was right back to her old ways, keeping secrets. It was like her relationship with Conall wasn't really happening. She couldn't talk about it, nor show him any affection in public.

If Conall Hamilton thought for one moment that he was going to have his way and not make an honest woman out of her, he'd better think again. She had been courted long enough.

A cool breeze blew past her. She shivered, her curls wafting into the wind. Conall was either going to do the honorable thing and ask her hand in marriage or she was moving on. No more secret meetings. No more flirting. And most of all, no more lovemaking. If he wanted her, he was going to make her his wife.

Although, her vow was most definitely going to be a hard one to keep. His storm-gray eyes raged with intensity every time he looked at her, capturing her. His body alone would be enough to tempt her beyond self-control. Tall and lean, muscles shaped his body to perfection. *A body built for sin*, she thought. Just the thought of him sent a wave of heat surging through her.

Indeed, it was going to be tough, for Conall was her savior. He'd saved her from self-destructing when she arrived at Black Stone. She had been a mess, never trusting anyone, most certainly men. She kept to herself, shutting everyone out. Being used by her brother in the evilest ways, it was a miracle that Conall had gotten through to her. Effie hung her head and her heart broke with the thought of losing her friend...her protector...her lover.

Though her secrets were her own to keep; she had never told him she was a Maxwell, nor did she tell him about the abuse. She was ashamed. And frankly, she'd lived that hell once, there was no need to do so again.

Furthermore, Conall would never marry a whore. He was an

honorable man, respected by all. A reputation like his should not be tarnished by her repulsive past.

Aye, the past was in the past. Knowing she would never have to return home to Caerlaverock Castle brought her relief. Her secrets were safe. Black Stone was her home now and she felt at peace. Whether he was going to ask for her hand in marriage or not, she had to make him see that she was far more valuable as a wife than a secret.

The reverberating sound of steel on steel reminded Effie she needed to retrieve the lock and key from the blacksmith. Making her way to the smith's shop, the smell of burning iron filled her senses. A chestnut ox stood outside the shop, wooly from his winter coat and blocking the entrance to the smithy.

"Shoo!" Effie demanded and waved her hands. The ox looked up at her, chewing its cud. The animal stood firm. Resorting to harsher means, she slapped his arse, and he moved. "Stubborn animal."

She knocked on the door. When no one answered, her patience wore thin. "For the love of saints." Effie rolled her eyes and knocked again.

Opening the door, she peeked in and saw the smith standing over a huge anvil hammering away as his sweat-soaked tunic clung to his muscled chest. He didn't notice Effie as she stood in the doorway. It was just like a craftsman to tune out the world when working.

"Excuse me!" Effie yelled over the clang of metal. Her body jumped with every hammer strike.

The smithy stopped, stood up straight, and turned toward Effie. "Och, lass, me morn just became brighter." He winked.

Effie smiled. "'Tis a good morn indeed, Rodrick."

Rodrick Carmichael laid his hammer aside and eyed her up and down with the devil twinkling in his eyes. "And what brings ye here?"

"I'm here for Alice's lock and key. Is it ready?"

"Aye." Rodrick wiped the sweat from his brow with the back of his arm. "Come in, I won't bite." A sly grin crept across his tanned face. "Unless ye want me to."

Daring to step over the threshold, Effie said, "Now, Rodrick

Carmichael, mind yer manners. That be no way to talk to a lady." She was used to dealing with arrogant Highlanders, and this man was no different. He had enough virility to make the ox outside envious.

Rodrick searched for Alice's lock. This gave Effie some time to look around the shop. A huge stone hearth took up most of the space, for the shop was small. One wooden workbench stood in the center of the room with various files and chisels scattered about. Different sized sledges and tongs neatly lined one side of the wall. *A true craftsman's workshop,* she thought.

A cot sat in a darkened corner with a small nightstand. As she viewed the cot, she wondered how life would be married to a blacksmith. Rodrick was the best at his craft. In fact, he provided the finest weapons throughout Scotland. This was why James had moved Rodrick closer to the castle and paid him generously.

Another benefit, he was easy on the eyes. Long black hair hung over his shoulders and his body was massive. A lass could drown if she stared too long in the deep blue depths of his eyes. But it wasn't just his ability to forge a magnificent sword or even his stunning features that made the people of Scotland talk. His reputation with the lasses was enough to raise caution. It would take an act of God to stop that man's wandering.

For Effie, he simply wasn't her Conall.

"Aye, here ye go, lass." Rodrick handed her the lock and key.

"Thank ye verra much. Alice will be pleased, I assure ye." Effie began to make her way to the door when Rodrick stopped her. "Ye dinnae have to leave so quickly."

"And why would ye want me to stay?"

Rodrick crossed his arms in front of his chest. "I would like to get to know ye better." He stumbled through his next words. "Nay, not in that way...but I want to know ye...Effie."

Cautious, Effie walked to the table, keeping her focus on the man. "There's no' much to know." She fumbled with a file on the worktable. "I'm just Effie."

"Och, lass. Ye be much more than ye think." Rodrick smiled.

Suddenly, the hammers and tongs began to rattle on the wall and the tools on the bench chattered as they danced across the wood. A loud clinking echoed as the fire poker came crashing down on the floor. The ground shook violently.

Panic pricked her spine as she felt herself lose balance. Before she hit the ground, she was pulled into a wall of hardened muscle as the blacksmith and Effie were thrown to the ground. Rodrick lay on top of her, shielding her from falling debris.

Even though the shaking had only lasted a brief moment, to Effie, it seemed like forever. Coughing from the dust, she struggled to breathe with the hulking Highlander pressed against her body. She felt every pebble from the ground dig deeper into her back. "Rodrick," she said, "I can no' breathe."

Rodrick's massive arms encaged her head as he leaned on his elbows, supporting his weight. "Are ye hurt?"

Effie swallowed hard past the dust in her throat. "Nay, I'm fine, but ye're squishing me."

The blacksmith stared down at Effie as if he was thinking about kissing her. His thumb brushed against her cheek.

Effie grew impatient with the man. "Rodrick Carmichael, get off of me!" She struggled beneath his weight.

"Effie, me and ye could be good together," he purred and kissed her cheek.

"Get off!" Effie pressed her palms into his chest, trying to shove him. What was wrong with him? They could have been hurt. "For the love of saints!"

The shop door flew open, breaking off its hinges, and Conall rushed in. He grabbed the smith by his tunic with both hands and threw him off Effie. Then he offered his hand to Effie.

She ignored it and glared at him. "What are ye doing here, Conall? Ye be following me?"

"We'll talk about this later." Conall stalked back to Rodrick until they were chest to chest. "The lady said to get off of her. Are yer ears working well today?"

"Ye broke me door!" The smith motioned to where said door used to be. "Ye will fix it!"

Effie dusted the dirt from her dress as she stood up. "I have had about enough of this...this barbaric nonsense!" She grabbed her basket and stormed out of the shop, leaving the men to their swinish bantering.

Once outside, the chill nipped at her skin. The earth had shaken, and all they could think about was fighting. *Absurd,* Effie thought as she pulled her cloak around her shoulders and strode toward the castle.

Worried about Abigale and her babe, she quickened her pace. The ground shakes were occurring often enough to cause worry. Even though the laird had reassured everyone not to, it still made the hairs bristle on the back of her neck.

A rough hand grabbed Effie's arm and spun her around. "Where are ye going?" Conall demanded.

"'Tis no concern of yers. Now release me."

"I'll let go if ye stop running from me."

"And what makes ye think I'm running? I do have better things to do than be concerned about ye." Effie was beyond frustrated with him, as well as the way the blacksmith had treated her. She had to take her anger out on someone and Conall just happened to be the one standing in front of her.

"God's wounds, Effie, haven't ye heard the rumors about the smith? Why would ye go into his shop alone? 'Tis like sending a lamb into a lion's den."

Effie snatched her arm out from his grip. "Are ye spying on me?" She looked at him crossly.

Conall stood with his hands on his hips with a sly grin on his face. Looking down, he kicked at a rock. "What be the matter, Effie? Ye know me better than that."

"I went to pick up a lock and key for —-"

"I know why ye were there, lass. I asked why ye would go inside his shop."

Effie narrowed her eyes at him. Was he thinking the worst of her? "Conall Hamilton, I can choose who I want to be with. I do no' need yer blessing. Furthermore, ye have no claim over me." Effie turned on her heels, but Conall wasn't letting her go. He spun her around again.

"Meet me at *our* place." A seriousness radiated from him that heated her to the core.

Effie gazed deeply into his eyes. "Conall Hamilton, I will no'..."

Conall cupped the back of her neck and pulled her closer until their lips were a mere whisper apart. "Meet me at our place." His voice was low and held a promise that she knew he would keep. A promise that kept her coming back for more every time. A promise of pleasure to come.

With a sly grin, Conall unpinned his cloak and handed it to Effie as he quit the bailey and trotted toward the glen's edge before she could protest. Truly she meant to stand firm and walk away, but the man drew her in and captivated her. She was his prisoner and his beautiful little secret.

3

Effie paced just outside the glen. Why couldn't she say no to this man? How was he supposed to take her seriously if she kept caving in to his every demand? Effie blew a strand of hair from her face and said, "I can no' believe what I'm about to do."

Yet, she could. Conall was the only man who made her feel alive. The way he bedded her was like nothing she had ever felt before. He savored every inch of her body, always coming back for more. It didn't matter how many times he made love to her, it always felt like the first time. She just wished she could talk about it, especially to Abigale and Alice.

Perhaps she was a wee bit jealous watching James and Abigale share their love for one another openly. They were inseparable. Abigale beamed about her husband's wicked ways and it only made her want to talk about Conall in the same light. It was only natural. Wasn't that what women did behind closed doors, gossip about their lovers?

The more she thought about it, the more she began to ache for Conall's touch. A need she felt right now warming her body. "For the love of saints!" The excitement was too much to hold back. Effie flung her basket to the ground, along with Conall's cloak, and raced deep into the forest.

Crunching leaves alerted Effie that he was there; he'd been waiting for her. Alas, he would have to wait a wee bit longer, for she wasn't ready to be caught. She hid behind a big yew tree. Her chest rose rapidly as she tried to suck in the cool air. The glen became eerily quiet. The ground trembled slightly and she grinned.

Although they had played this game of cat and mouse numerous times, the thrill was still there nipping at her stomach. The rules of the game were simple; if she could reach the circle of stones first, she was safe, but if he caught her, she was his for the taking.

Convinced that Conall was still a distance off, Effie ran toward the stones. Her cloak whipped behind her as she pumped her legs as fast as she could, weaving between the trees. She knew the path so well. *Almost there.* Just around the bend and she would reach the circle.

He stalked her like wild game, even though he was out of sight. Knowing it was a bad idea to take her eyes off the stones, she dared to glance behind her. When she turned back she came to an abrupt stop. She smiled. It was Conall.

A huge storm-gray dragon stood before her. Massive horns proudly perched on top of the dragon's head and seemed to touch the sky. His scales glistened as a ray of sunlight burst through the trees and shined upon him. He folded his wings as he approached her.

"Ye're late," Conall growled deeply. Although his mouth didn't move, Effie could hear him through mind-speak, as if he was a part of her being.

Through labored breaths Effie replied, "Nay, ye were a wee bit slow in catching me this time. I do believe I almost outwitted the dragon." Effie smirked and removed her cloak.

Conall laughed, which was more like a deep belly-rumble, and began to circle her. Warm air from his nostrils blew down her neck, making her heart thump faster. She closed her eyes and prayed that he wouldn't make her wait long.

"Aye, lass, I thought ye might have changed yer mind and went home."

"I wanted to, but me legs didnae want to move in that direction." Effie seductively unlaced the front of her dress as she looked up into the dragon's eyes. They flashed blue with intensity.

Conall bent his head down and brushed up against her chest. "I'm glad ye came."

Effie took a step back and her dress pooled at her feet. Her curly red hair hid her breasts as she stood in front of the dragon as naked as the day she was born.

For the briefest moment, the cold air caused her to shiver and her teeth began to chatter. The dragon felt her discomfort and quickly wrapped his tail around her waist, pulling her closer. Rough scales brushed against her skin, sending an erotic sensation through her body. *For the love of saints! When is he going to shift?*

Building anticipation was the torturous part of the game they loved. The more he held back, the more she craved his touch.

Her body pressed against his warm chest as she caressed his silvery scales. They were perfect for shielding against arrows. Yet, soft when touched the right way.

In a flash, the dragon's tail disappeared. Now it was the flesh and blood Conall standing before her. Naked and perfect.

His stormy gaze took in every inch of her body, as if he was making love to her with his eyes. She trembled as he licked his lips and approached her. Strong, powerful hands gripped the sides of her head, pulling her into a ravenous, soul-crushing kiss. Effie wrapped her arms around his neck. As he warmed her with the heat radiating from his skin, the cold was soon forgotten.

He kissed her again and again.

Who was she fooling? She could never leave Conall. No mortal man could ever compare, he was her dragon to love, even if she had to stay a secret.

∽

With her back against the tree, Conall thrust deep into Effie and knew he wouldn't be able to last long. *Holy hell!* Seeing the blacksmith with Effie was enough to set his dragon flying off the cliffs of jealousy and into a sea of impulsive desire to stake his claim, and not just physically. *Bastard!* Not only did he have his wife's ghost pressuring him to marry the lass, now his dragon was adding his opinion. In fact, he didn't recall asking the beastie for his blessing.

Feeling her legs tighten around his hips, he knew his red-haired lass was close to crumbling in his arms. Off to the side, he saw her cloak piled on the ground. Conall moved them over to the spot and laid her down. She stared up at him, her vibrant eyes as green as the glen's grass in spring. He brushed the back of his hand against her cheek. There was much more to their relationship than he realized. Had it been there all along? He felt like he was seeing her for the first time, the true woman who had stolen his heart.

"Conall, what be the matter with ye?"

He smiled down at her. "Be me wife." He didn't know where the words had come from. Hell, he didn't care. Perhaps this morning's pondering had finally become clear to him. He wanted Effie to be his wife.

"Yer wife?" Effie's forehead creased in disbelief.

"Aye." Conall thrust deeply inside her again, making her moan. She arched beneath him.

"Finally ye're going to make an honest woman out of me?" she teased.

Conall stilled and held her stare. "I've never questioned yer honesty. 'Tis me I question. I failed me last marriage. I dinnae want to fail ye."

Effie tightened her legs around his waist and took his head in her hands. "Ye could never fail me, Conall. Ye saved me."

"Then ye'll be me wife?"

She was holding back the tears; he could tell by the way her chin wrinkled and her bottom lip quivered. Before he knew it, she'd flashed him the brightest smile he had ever seen. "Aye."

Conall pressed deeper inside her, pumping hard and fast. The passion grew into a fevered pitch, causing them to crash through the walls of ecstasy together.

After, he nuzzled her neck, relishing the honey scent of her hair. Christ, he needed this woman more than the air he breathed. Everything about her drove him mad. Her boldness amused him, her intelligence intrigued him, her beauty was beyond temptation, but most of all, Effie was strong; she was a survivor.

As Effie cuddled up in Conall's arms, he kissed down her neck and between her breasts.

"When shall we marry?" she asked.

Conall rolled over on his side, propping himself up on his elbow. His free hand roamed her body. "James needs me to oversee a situation. Something about cattle raiding of some sort. I shall be no longer than three nights. Will that give ye enough time to prepare?" He grinned.

"Ye're giving me three days to prepare our wedding?" Effie said, shocked.

"How much time do ye need? Ye get the priest, put on a dress," Conall shrugged his shoulders, "and be done with it."

Effie playfully slapped at his chest. "If that's what it takes to get ye in front of the priest, then it shall be done."

Conall leaned over and kissed her. "As far as I'm concerned, ye be me wife already. I do no' need a priest's blessing."

For the rest of the afternoon and into the evening, they stayed wrapped in each other's arms until the threat of cold crept up on them. Effie tried to escape Conall's arms but was quickly stopped. "Where do ye think ye're going?"

Effie loved the fact that he didn't want to let her go; however, the cold pricked at her skin and she began to shiver. "I'm getting dressed, 'tis cold."

Conall pulled her closer, and she instantly warmed up.

"Conall, I have to start planning our wedding. Dinnae ye think we should be getting back?"

"Nay." He kissed her neck.

"Ye're distracting me." She pushed at his chest.

"Aye." Ignoring her, Conall continued the sweet kissing-assault down her chest and captured a nipple with his mouth.

For the love of saints, this man drove her daft. She supposed that he was getting his fill of her before he left for three days. *Three days.* Arranging a wedding in so short a time would be challenging. But she had Abigale and Alice to help her. Effie sat up as Conall huffed his disapproval. "I have little time to plan our wedding. I can no' stay here any longer."

Effie stood and grabbed her dress. She was glad that next time he bedded her, they would be in a warm room under furs on a proper bed, not under an old yew tree out in the cold. Though, as she looked around the forest, she knew this place would always be their special secret. She thought herself lucky the woodland creatures couldn't talk.

"Well, are ye coming with me, or are ye staying out here to freeze?" Effie asked.

"Och lass, did ye bring me cloak?"

Shite! In her passion-filled frenzy she had forgotten she'd dropped everything when she ran into the glen. "I left it along with me basket at the edge of the woods."

Conall smiled and shook his head. "Looks like I'll be escorting ye back to grab me cloak then. I have no clothes with me."

Effie blushed. Of course, he didn't have any clothes. He had shifted. "Here, take this." She offered him her cloak so at least he could cover up.

"Nay, ye'll freeze. I'll be fine, dinnae fash yerself." Conall stood and draped her cloak over her shoulders. "Let's go fetch me clothes."

As they crunched through the dry old leaves, Effie couldn't

believe that she was going to be a wife. Conall was her perfect prince. She looked up at him and they shared a smile. *Three days.* She could wait that long.

They reached the clearing and Effie quickly fetched her basket with Conall's cloak. She dared one last look at his naked body.

"Ye know lass, yer quite bonny when ye blush like that. Yer freckles darken." Conall walked up to her and cupped her face, kissing her cheeks. "I have something for ye."

Effie rolled her eyes. "Conall, I told ye I have to go." Her attention was instantly brought to her hand. A golden ring with joined hands had been slipped on her finger. She looked up at Conall in surprise.

"This is so everyone knows ye're spoken for."

"'Tis beautiful."

"Aye, it fits ye perfectly."

Indeed, it did. Effie's dreams were coming true.

4

"Sir Herbert de Maxwell, a courageous, knighted warrior, a true faithful subject of the crown, and chief of Clan Maxwell," Tavish addressed his dying father. "A warden of the Scottish West March, you've kept this side of the March firmly. The bravest amongst his people, vowed to protect his clan and family with his life. You are adored by many." Tavish sat deep in thought with his hands steepled under his chin in a dark corner of a bedchamber.

"Aye, indeed a true hero," he spat. He remembered a time when the fallen man had been strong and in good health. Standing over six feet tall with broad shoulders and a battle scar marring his left cheek, the good knight had been the epitome of a Highlander.

But Tavish knew the man's true nature. Growing up under the chief's rule had made Tavish who he was today; a cunning, cruel man who was evil to the core. Even though his father recognized him as his own, it didn't mean he loved his son. In fact, Tavish felt like a ghost around his father most of the time. He understood he was an outsider but being dismissed was like a knife to his gut. It stung. At a very young age he had realized he was on his own and had to fight for what he wanted.

Indeed, living a lie was something he guessed they both had in common. Tavish was nothing more than an intruder to their perfect noble family. He saw it every day in his stepmother's eyes. The hurt she harbored about his father's infidelity shone through her cold, blue eyes, especially when the wee brat came along. Though she had long forgiven her husband, it was Tavish whom she held responsible for Herbert's actions. Adultery was a strong brew to swallow.

In the townsfolk's eyes, Clan Maxwell was an honorable, loving family, but behind closed doors the truth was painfully obvious.

Tavish slowly stood. No sleep for days had left his eyes bloodshot and his mood foul. He walked over to his dying father's bedside. He tucked the fur around his frail body. The man coughed and wheezed, fighting to breathe air into his decayed lungs. The once healthy man was now dying. He was pale and thin, his hair gray, sparse, and brittle to the touch. "Yet here ye lie. A corpse."

Once his father's lungs began to disease, he knew it wouldn't be long before death would come for Sir Herbert. Tavish had visited his father every day since he fell ill, praying for the words he longed to hear from him. Yet, deep inside he knew those words would never come. "All I ever wanted was yer love, da." He wiped the blood from the auld man's lips.

Eyeing a goose-feather pillow lying on top of a trunk at the foot of the bed, Tavish walked over and picked it up. He fluffed it. "I must say, ye've taught me one valuable lesson in life. Would ye like to know what it is?" Tavish walked back to his father's bedside while flipping the pillow back and forth from hand to hand. "I reckon ye would." He leaned down and whispered in his ear, "If ye want something, it be up to yerself to take it."

Tavish stood over the bed and relished the fear he saw in his father's eyes. He felt nothing but pure hatred toward the man. With one last flip of the pillow, he stared deeply into the dying man's eyes and said coldly, "I may be a bastard in yer eyes but I'm the one who made ye a legend. 'Tis time for a new chief."

Quickly, Tavish covered Herbert's face with the pillow. There wasn't much of a fight. After he felt the last twitch of his father's body, he removed the pillow. Tavish closed the dead man's eyes and threw the pillow in the hearth, watching it go up in flames. There was no remorse, just satisfaction of a job well done.

Once outside, Tavish closed the bedchamber door and nodded to a man on guard. "'Tis done."

Both men walked together down a long corridor. "Have ye sent a message to yer sister?" Sir Henry asked.

"Aye."

"Good."

The man stopped Tavish in mid-stride with concern on his face. "How are ye going to convince yer sister? She's going to ask a lot of questions. She's going to want to know why ye didnae call for her sooner."

"Ye dinnae have to fash yerself over me sister," Tavish reassured him. "I can handle her. All ye have to do is play yer part and we shall both reap the benefits." He placed his hand on the knight's shoulder and squeezed.

"Aye." Sir Henry nodded, and they both continued down the corridor. "Ye know our agreement, and I would hate to have to go back on my word if ye fail me."

Over-confident, Tavish straightened his frame. "No need to think about such drastic measures. I've assured ye, me sister will be here. Trust me."

As they rounded a corner, a maid ran into the men. "Please, excuse me." She bowed her head and looked to the ground. "Yer guests have arrived."

A wicked smile crept across Tavish's face as he looked at his partner in crime. "Very well, Maggie."

Very well indeed.

∼

Uneasiness churned Conall's gut as he and ten of his trusted men were escorted to the great hall of Caerlaverock Castle. It wasn't the stale bread and cheese he had for breakfast. His dragon was restless and should have warned him.

It didn't make sense why he was there. Clan Maxwell had been allies with Clan Douglas, even fought alongside King Robert the Bruce. Yet he felt on edge. Being that the castle was moated by stagnant water from the heavy rainfall, there was only one entrance and exit, which left the Dragonkine warrior and his men an easy target.

The Maxwell stronghold was a vision of wealth and power. Once past the twin tower gatehouse and cramped stairway, the castle opened up to a spacious courtyard where Maxwell folk milled around, carrying out their daily duties. Red sandstone-bricks surrounded them, and off in the distance he could hear the crying of larks.

As Conall and his men made their way through the courtyard, villagers eyed them cautiously. Conall had a strange feeling these folks did not take easily to outsiders.

One of his men, Broc, walked next to him with his hand on the hilt of his sword. "I dinnae believe we are welcome here."

Conall kept his gaze focused in front of him, on alert. "Aye, Broc, keep yer sword ready."

Broc was a younger lad of eight-and-ten, tall as Conall, built like a stone wall, and one hell of a warrior. Conall knew the lad's family and he had taken Broc under his wing and trained the boy well. He knew if attacked, Broc would prevail.

The escort led the men into the great hall where a long wooden table stood. The hearth was blazing with a fire and a kitchen maid busied herself placing provisions out on the table for their guests.

"Help yerselves. The laird will be here shortly," the escort informed them.

Conall couldn't stop thinking about Effie. In fact, she had been on his mind throughout the trip to Dumfries. Each day he spent away from her he grew more irritated. Conall had a good head on his shoulders, for the most part. As long as he knew he had Effie, he felt like he could conquer anything or any man that got in his way. Eyeing his surroundings, he grew more annoyed by the moment.

Although the plan had been for James to make this trip instead of Conall, he couldn't allow his best friend to go and leave Abigale alone and pregnant. God forbid if something happened to her and James wasn't there to defend her. It was the natural choice for Conall to go. If he rode hard and fast through the night, he would be home and buried deep inside his redheaded-lass in less than a day. If he had his way, he would shift and be there in half the time.

He joined his men and was eating a few bites of cheese when the double doors to the great hall opened, sending Conall and his men-at-arms to attention. Two guards stood by the door as a few of Maxwell's men walked in and took their seats.

A man who exuded authority walked in and approached Conall. "Tavish Maxwell." He nodded his head in greeting.

"Conall Hamilton. Me men and I are here on behalf of Laird James Douglas." Conall nodded. "We are here to meet with Sir Herbert. We have business to discuss."

Tavish scratched his chin. "Aye. Please sit." He motioned for Conall to take a seat.

Conall sat across from Tavish and next to Broc. The young warrior leaned into Conall. "Something is no' right here."

"Aye." Conall nodded. Indeed, something felt wrong but he couldn't put his finger on it.

"It saddens me to report that Sir Herbert won't be joining us today," Tavish said.

This was odd. Why didn't the laird want to meet with him? Perhaps he was seeing to other business.

"Are ye here in his place?"

"Aye. I'm his son. Now, what business can I assist ye with?"

"It has been brought to Laird Douglas's attention that someone in your clan has been blackmailing Clan Lockheart."

Tavish sat back in his chair and crossed his arms over his chest as Conall continued.

"The Lockheart's, your neighbors to the east, are paying ye an extra amount of coin for protection when in fact the clan is already under the protection of Clan Douglas. This agreement between Clan Maxwell and Clan Lockheart was made after a significant amount of cattle had gone missing."

"Och, when has being under the protection of James the Black Douglas done any good? As ye can see for yerself, our tower to the north was almost seized and now lies in ruins. I do no' recall a Douglas running to our defense when the English tried to take our home."

At this point, Conall could feel the irritation stirring inside him. Not only was this smug arse a thief but a liar to boot. At no point had Sir Herbert requested Clan Douglas's help, furthermore, they had not been aware of an attack.

"'Tis not the issue at hand, Tavish. Ye can no' blackmail the Lockhearts. They can no' pay yer fees and they need their cattle to survive."

Tavish laughed and leaned in, resting his arms on the table. "So, James sends ye to keep the peace, aye? The laird's messenger," he chuckled.

With all his resolve, Conall held back his anger and the urge to rip the bastard's head off his shoulders. The wee shite was quickly becoming a thistle in his backside.

"Tavish, replace the stolen cattle and stop the harassment or…"

"Or what? Please do tell," the cocky bastard bit back.

"james will have no choice in the matter but to involve King Robert."

Hastily Tavish stood, and his men-at-arms followed, causing Conall and his men to do the same.

"I have no loyalty to King Robert," spat Tavish. "Me allegiance stands with King Edward."

This new-found information stunned Conall. He never would have thought that the Maxwell's were backbiters. The tension in the air was thick, and Conall could sense Tavish's hostility toward him.

"And at what cost, Tavish? Was it worth the price?" Conall spat, disgusted by how easily humans fell into temptation.

"Och, the gains will benefit me greatly, I assure ye." With that said, Tavish placed his empty tankard upside down on the table.

As if on cue, the men on both sides drew their swords and stood in battle stance, waiting for someone to make the first move. There was no doubt blood was going to be shed today. Conall had hoped it wouldn't come to this. Yet he couldn't help but think that this whole awkward situation had been a setup.

Tavish pointed his sword at Conall's neck. "Men, I do believe we have found me father's murderer."

Astounded, Conall took a step back. "Yer father? Murdered?"

"Aye, Sir Herbert was me father and is now dead."

The doors to the great hall slammed shut, trapping his men. War cries rang out and the sound of clanging steel echoed about the room. Conall was hit from behind, causing him to lose focus on Tavish.

If a fight was what they wanted, then so be it. He wasn't going to accept blame, nor be accused of a crime he had not committed.

Conall swung his sword around and connected with his assailant, stabbing him in the gut. From the corner of his eye, he saw Tavish making a mad dash toward the door. The coward was trying to escape.

Running toward the exit and leaping over a fallen chair, he caught up to the bastard. "And where do ye think ye be going?" Conall grabbed the back of Tavish's tunic and threw him to the ground.

With the sword pressed into the eejit's neck, Conall stood over Tavish. "Ye know as well as I, I didnae commit murder. Ye will halt yer attack and allow me men to go."

Tavish smiled wickedly as a Maxwell stood behind Conall with a blade to his throat. How easily could one's fate change? Feeling the cold steel pressed into his skin calmed the raging dragon inside him and Conall dropped his weapon. Though immortal, the only way to kill a Dragonkine was to behead them, so treading softly would suit him well. No need to lose your head, especially by a human.

Tavish stood and dusted his trews as if nothing had happened. He had the upper hand now. As he approached Conall, he unsheathed his dirk.

Conall struggled against his captor's hold, yet the steel held him back. Tavish stood face to face with him and whispered in his ear, "Dinnae forget, ye be on me land." The bastard stabbed Conall in the chest with his dirk, then turned and faced his men. "Please show our guest hospitality and lead him to his room." With his last order made, Tavish quit the great hall.

Stinging pain ripped through Conall's chest and his knees threatened to buckle. God's wounds! How was he going to get out of there? The only way out was to shift, and quite frankly, he wasn't willing to take the risk. Too many people would witness his change. Aye, going dragon right now was a bad idea.

He looked over at Broc as he was being led by two guards toward the great hall. He'd been badly wounded, yet was still alive. Most of his men weren't that lucky; they had been brutally murdered. The future looked grim for the Highlander.

5

"Och, my lady, I do believe the wee one has grown a bit," Alice huffed as she bunched up all the extra material she could gather around Abigale's waist.

Being pregnant, Abigale's belly was growing bigger every day, causing her dresses to be uncomfortable. If it wasn't for Alice and her sewing skills, she would have had no choice but to grab a sheet and alter it to her liking. She supposed she could cut a hole for her head and just let the rest of the material hang where it may. At this point, Abigale cared naught about appearances; she wanted comfort.

Looking down, she also noticed another body part expanding. Her bosom. Although it kept her husband pleasantly content at night, her back was protesting all the extra weight. Not to mention the swelling in her feet. Most days she was barefoot, for her shoes were too tight.

Everything was too tight. Her whole body felt like it was going to explode.

"Alice, I dinnae know what to do." Abigale held her arms high as Alice fussed over the woolen fabric. "This babe must be a boy, I'm constantly eating. At breakfast, I ate more than Rory." She placed her hands on her swollen belly. "And half of James's pudding. Alice, I'm going to pop!"

"Ye'd best no' be popping just yet," said Alice. "'Tis perfectly normal, me dear." Alice winked at her.

Effie smiled as she watched Alice fuss over Abigale. She was happy for her best friend, truly. Yet in a way, Effie was envious. She wanted a husband to love her as much as the laird loved his wife and to be able to tell the world about it.

Effie watched as Alice took a step back to view her creation. Bearing children with the man she loved would be the greatest gift of all. *Soon*, she thought, *verra soon*.

A loud knock on Abigale's bedchamber door brought Effie's attention back from the clouds. As she opened the door, two wee blonde girls rushed in. They had been abandoned and living in unsavory conditions when Abigale had rescued them from the village months ago. Still, no one had claimed them and now the sisters called Black Stone on the Hill their home. Abigale and James treated them as their own children.

Little, if any, information had been known about the girls. At first, the eldest did not trust easily, but when she came around, Abigale was able to learn their names. Flora was the eldest, and Annis, the youngest. She remained a wee girl with her own ideas and a strong personality. Aye, Annis was quite a handful. Though she had yet to speak, she communicated quite well. And her sister, of course, her protector, had grown into a fine young lass.

Effie was about to close the door when she nearly shut it on Laird Douglas. "My laird, please forgive me. I did no' see ye there."

Standing over six feet tall, James walked in the room. Holding a piece of rolled parchment in his hands he said, "Good day, Effie. This came for ye this morn." He handed the missive to her, then walked toward Abigale.

Effie closed the door and fumbled with the seal. Who could possibly send word to her? Unless, oh dear God, nay. As she opened the scroll, thoughts of Conall rushed into her mind. What if he was in some kind of trouble? He had to be safe and alive, he just had to be.

Sending a prayer to God, she quickly flattened the paper and began to read.

The chamber began to spin. If father had found her, so had Tavish.

"Effie!" Abigale ran over to her and walked her to a chair near the hearth. "Alice, bring her some wine."

Alice rushed to Effie. "Here dear, drink."

Effie drained the tankard. She'd need more wine to settle her nerves.

In bold black letters the scroll stated that she was needed back home, and a man would be waiting downstairs to escort her to Caerlaverock Castle. Signed by her father, Sir Herbert Maxwell.

Home.

Shocked, Effie leaned back into the chair. She hadn't been back home in over five years and had hoped to never return.

Why did her father want her home? Was he ill? Perhaps something had happened to Tavish. Surely her father would have mentioned that type of information in the note?

Mayhap Conall wasn't on business after all. *That's it*, Effie thought. Could Conall have found out who her father was and gone to him to ask for her hand in marriage, to bless the marriage? He would be there waiting for her while making necessary arrangements to marry her at the castle in front of her family. *For the love of saints*, she hoped not. If Tavish was there, he would make damn sure to tell Conall all about her past and ruin everything she'd kept a secret all these years.

Effie's heart raced and she began to panic. Taking in a deep breath, she tried to calm her rattled nerves. *Breathe Effie, breathe. There's no way he could find out unless... Alice.* Alice was the only one who knew her last name. Surely Conall did not know she was a Maxwell? It was really quite silly for her to even think that he was at Caerlaverock. Alice had promised to never share her secret. She remembered the day quite well...

She had been back at Caerlaverock, waking from a fog. Her head pounded, her body ached, and her face was numb. Sitting up slowly through the shooting pain, Effie opened one eye, for the other was swollen shut. As her surroundings became visible, she noticed she was lying in hay with the smell of horse manure and soiled straw lingering in the air. She must be in the stables. But how had she gotten there?

Aye, she recalled the recent beating her brother had doled out to her, but as for how she made it to the stables, that remained a mystery. All she knew was, enough was enough. She refused to allow her body to be used again by some drunken lout Tavish had promised her to. There was no desire in bedding a man whose breath reeked of ale and who only wanted to pleasure himself. The idea sickened her.

Regaining her strength, she sat up, observing the stables. She had grown dangerously numb. Going through each day in a fog was the only way she knew how to deal with life. On the other hand, it was how she protected herself. She no longer recognized the woman she had become.

When she had refused a man who was heavy in the pockets and belly, Tavish was beyond irate with her and made sure she knew it.

His rage came down fist by fist and blow by blow. She must have blacked out from the pain. His shouting and screaming rang through her head.

"Ye be me whore!" Tavish pushed her into her bedchamber. "When I say ye'll bed a man, ye'll do as I say!" He slapped her face, splitting her lip.

"Nay, Tavish! I can no' do it anymore!" Effie fought back but it was no use. The fire in her brother's eyes was lit. She was going to pay dearly for her disobedience.

"Whore! Do ye want me to tell father about yer lover?" He punched her so hard in the face, she staggered back until she fell to the ground.

Now she was in the stables, rocking back and forth, trying to forget everything. Aye, she'd had enough.

Surely a guardian angel had protected her, brought her there.

Aye, she would miss her da, but if she stayed, she was as good as dead. Leaving would set her free. As close as she was to her da, he would forgive her leaving without a goodbye. Bedding a man before marriage was something her father would not easily overlook.

Tavish could still blackmail her if he found her. She didn't want to think about the consequences. All she wanted was freedom. With that in mind,

Effie eyed a chestnut mare. The mare with kind eyes glanced back at her as if reassuring her to move forward with her plan. The question was, would she be able to leave Dumfries alive?

In order to stand, she grabbed the chestnut around her neck for support. A cold wet nose nudged Effie, encouraging her to keep moving. Taking in a deep breath, she flung her leg over the mare's back and settled herself. She kicked the horse into motion and hung on for dear life, praying that they would make it out of Dumfries alive.

With only the clothes on her back and a fatigued mare, Effie, by the grace of God, found herself on Douglas land. As she reached Black Stone, she could no longer hang onto her horse and fell onto the ground.

When she woke, it was to a gray-haired woman tending to her wounds.

"Where am I?" Effie asked.

"Black Stone on the Hill, lass. And ye be safe here."

"Who are ye?"

"Me name is Alice. I'm laird Douglas's eyes and ears around here." *She paused as she wiped the blood from the corner of Effie's mouth.* *"Now it be me turn to ask the questions. Who are ye and who did this to ye, lass?"*

Effie hesitated, wondering if she should tell her the truth. Douglas land was safe, that she knew by the way her father talked about Clan Douglas. They were allies.

"Look, lass, I know ye've run into some kind of trouble. These kinds of wounds tell a tale." Alice studied Effie intently as she waited for an answer.

Desperate to stay, Effie had to tell Alice everything, well almost everything. No one needed to know the extent of her past. Plus, Alice looked like she always got her way.

"If I tell ye who I am, can ye promise me that I can stay here?"

"Aye."

"Me name is Effie Maxwell and I seek protection."

"Lass, yer secret is safe with me as long as there be no trouble. We are in need of another hand around here, especially in the kitchens. Are ye able to work the kitchen?"

"Aye. I'll do whatever ye wish as long as ye dinnae send me back home."

"Well then, Effie Douglas, consider Black Stone yer home."

Relief like she had never felt before washed over her broken and beaten body. She had a home. As tears streamed down her face, the realization that she had a new life was too much for Effie to comprehend at the moment. She knew the road ahead was going to be hard. She had a lot of healing to do. Making a promise to herself, she vowed to never look back, for tonight she became *Effie Douglas*.

"Effie. Please say something." Abigale's voice brought her back to the present.

"I'm fine," Effie said.

"Oh, thank God!" Abigale blew out a breath in relief. "I thought ye had gone into some kind of shock."

Perhaps she had. Unfortunately, it seemed her past was catching up with her.

"I did no' mean to worry ye. I skipped breakfast this morn and I feel a wee bit ill. 'Tis all. I'll be fine," Effie said.

She had been so busy she'd forgotten to tell Alice and Abigale about her betrothal. A smile spread across her face as she looked from Alice to Abigale, who were hovering over her. "I'm getting married."

Silence filled the room. Alice and Abigale appeared dumbfounded by her news.

"Married?" Alice asked.

"Conall asked me to be his wife." Effie beamed.

Abigale squealed and clapped her hands. "When's the wedding?"

"In two days, but I just got a message from me da, he wants me to come home."

"Did he say why?" Alice asked with a concerned look.

"Nay, but I must leave now."

"Are ye sure? Do ye want someone to go with ye? I can ask Rory since Conall is no' here," Alice offered.

Effie saw how nervous Alice became when she mentioned returning home. By the look on Alice's face, she did not want Effie to go back to Dumfries.

"I'll be fine, Alice. No need to involve Rory. As much as I love his company," Effie said sarcastically, "I'll pass. Besides, Father has sent an escort."

Abigale looked down at her belly and rubbed it.

"Oh Abigale, I'll be back before the babe is born," Effie promised.

"Good, I can no' go through the birth without ye." Abigale smiled.

Effie quit the room and was walking down the corridor when Alice caught up to her.

"Effie," Alice called out. "I dinnae like this plan of yers."

Effie stopped and turned around. "I have no choice."

"I find it odd that the message didnae say why ye'er needed at home. Either ye're no' telling me something or this is trickery."

"I'm telling the truth. All it says is that me father needs me. If he's fallen ill I must go to him, Alice. I never said goodbye." The words lodged in Effie's throat as she fought back tears.

"Och, lass." Alice wrapped her arms around her. "I understand but 'tis dangerous to go back home. Something does no' feel right. I learned long ago to trust those instincts. I dinnae want to see ye hurt."

"I have to go now." Effie ignored Alice's warning. This was something she had to do no matter how much she didn't want to. Effie pulled out of her embrace. "I'll be back soon. I promise."

"I dinnae like this. I smell a rat and he be yer brother."

"Please, Alice."

Alice tsked and placed her hands on her hips. "I should lock ye in yer chamber and stop this nonsense. However, I'm no' yer mother." Alice pressed her lips together, concern spread across her face. "If ye're no' back in two days, I'm sending for ye." She hugged Effie again, clinging to her as if it was the last time she'd see her. "Be careful, lass."

~

The earthy smell of marshland mixed with the salty sea breeze welcomed her as approached Caerlaverock Castle. A flock of sea larks hovered over the castle gliding on the wind, spiraling toward the heavens. A storm was on the way.

The day's journey had started out before sunrise and now was ending just as evening approached. The rain had held off most of the day and now a light drizzle fell, leaving Effie cold and damp.

The closer she got to Dumfries, old memories flooded over her. Some she held dear, others she wished she could forget.

When her mum died of fever, Effie had been ten-and-eight. The emptiness she felt at losing her was unbearable, so she depended on her da more and more. They had grown extremely close. Being overly protective of his daughter, Sir Herbert never pushed the idea of marriage. He was perfectly content to have Effie home and by his side. Looking back, she could see why. He had mourned his wife terribly; they both had. Effie was all that he had left to remind him of his wife. Life had been comfortable then, until the day she'd met the lad she was going to marry, William.

William was a neighboring clan chief's son, tall, dark, and wickedly handsome. The moment she bumped into him at the market, it was lust at first sight. How quickly William had turned her into a wanton lass, she thought. In no time at all, they were scampering off to secluded places to be alone.

Effie stopped her horse just shy of the twin-towered gatehouse. Memories flashed before her of William, down on bended knee, asking her hand in marriage. It was supposed to be the happiest day of her life. As they were celebrating in the stables, wrapped up in passion, Tavish found them. To this day, Tavish's mischievous face still branded her memories.

Tavish seized the opportunity. He couldn't allow Effie to marry nor be happy. He needed something to hold against her so she would do his dirty work. He reassured her he would keep her premarital bedding a secret, but she would have to obey his every command. At the time she had no choice, it would kill her father if he ever found out. Knowing now just how much it had cost her, she wished she had rethought her options.

She never knew what happened to William. He never called upon her again. Effie shook her head, trying to forget the past. It was time to be brave and walk through the gates of her childhood home.

There was a part of her that wished her dragon was there to

protect her. But that hope slipped away, for she knew it was silly to believe such nonsense. Conall could not have found out her true identity.

She passed beneath the arching entrance of the gatehouse. *What has happened here?* When she had left, the castle was kept in respectable condition. Now the stones were covered in moss and lichen. And the bridge leading to the gatehouse had cracks in the foundation.

As she rode across the bridge, she noticed the north tower, once a powerful stronghold, lay in ruins as if it had been attacked.

As she came to the gatehouse, she was greeted by a stable hand who took her horse.

"Good eve, Mistress Maxwell!"

Maxwell? She almost didn't recognize her auld name. She hadn't been called a Maxwell in so long.

A man she recognized all too well approached her. "Sir Neil, 'tis good to see ye." Effie greeted him with a warm smile. Not only had the knight been close to her father and a trusted friend, he was the commander of the Maxwell war band. "Where's Father?"

The Highlander appeared too grim. "'Tis best ye rest and eat. I'll escort ye to yer chamber."

Effie followed Neil to her bedchamber, praying she wouldn't see Tavish along the way. Quickly, she was regretting her decision to come home.

6

The frigid chill of winter bit through Effie's bedchamber as she woke with a shiver. Pulling the furs closer, she snuggled deeper into her bed, not wanting to get up. She'd meant to take a short rest after her bath last night, then meet her father for the last meal, but she'd fallen asleep.

The door groaned open and she could hear someone's soft footsteps enter her chamber.

"Conall!" Effie quickly sat up.

"Nay, my lady. 'Tis me, Maggie." The chambermaid busied herself stacking wood next to the hearth.

Effie plopped back down into the bed, disappointed that her visitor wasn't Conall. She must have been dreaming. Aye, a beautiful dream.

"Good morn, my lady."

Effie stretched her arms high over her head. "Good morn." She yawned. She couldn't remember the last time she had slept so soundly.

Effie looked about her childhood chamber; it hadn't changed much. Spacious with colorful rugs placed neatly on the floor, matching tapestries hung proudly on the walls. One stood out from the rest, one she was happy to see. She'd made it for her mother as she laid in her bed dying of fever. It was of a wee girl holding her mother's hand as angels looked down upon them from the heavens above. Effie remembered wrapping her mother in the tapestry believing the angels would protect her. Effie closed her eyes, holding back the tears. *I miss ye, mum.*

When her eyes opened, a white sheet covering an oddly-shaped object on a chair, came into view. Effie flung her feet over the side of the bed and stood. Wrapping the fur around her shivering body, she walked over to the chair and pulled the sheet off.

The gold shined anew, the strings were tight, and the embedded Celtic knot work was still unforgettable. It was her harp. Running her hand over the strings, her fingers ached to play.

Whenever she felt lonely or sad, Effie would lose herself behind the harp. The escape brought her clarity.

"I have a fresh gown and shoes for ye." The chambermaid brought the dress over to her.

"I thank ye kindly." Effie took the green woolen dress from the lass; it was one of her favorites.

"Will ye be needing help?"

"Nay, I shall be fine."

The maid never made eye contact with her. Effie couldn't stop thinking that perhaps Tavish had something to do with Maggie being so timid. She was young and attractive, a perfect victim for her brother to take advantage of.

"Maggie, has me brother harmed ye in any way?"

The chambermaid stood silent.

"Ye can tell me. I can keep ye safe."

"Mistress, yer brother has been kind to me."

Seeing the dark circles under her eyes and the way she was avoiding eye contact, Effie knew Maggie was lying. "I know how horrible he can be. Ye seem like a nice lass, Maggie."

"Is there anything else I can help ye with?" The chambermaid squared her shoulders and glared Effie.

Effie sensed the maid was keeping something form her. Had Tavish already hurt her? "I know me brother is mean. I can help ye."

Maggie walked past her to straighten the pillows on the bed, ignoring her.

For Maggie's sake, Effie prayed she'd trust her.

Effie dressed quickly, eager to speak with her father. Sitting down at her dressing table, she brushed out her curly hair. After years of living with the guilt of never saying goodbye to her da, she knew it wouldn't be an easy task to ask for his forgiveness. It must have hurt him terribly the way she had left.

Being home had a strange effect on her. She knew it was time to be completely honest with the people she loved, especially Conall. He deserved to know the truth about the woman he was about to marry. She was ready to start anew with her father and Conall. It gave her hope for a better future. If all else failed, she could marry the blacksmith.

Once she finished her hair, settling on pulling it back from her face and securing it with a leather cord, she stood. Dizziness overcame her and she braced herself with a hand on the back of the chair. Either her nerves were getting the best of her or it was hunger. She needed food.

"Are ye all right?" Maggie rushed over.

"Aye, I stood up too fast, 'tis all." Effie smiled at the maid. "I'm a wee bit hungry."

~

The great hall was humming with clan Maxwell's elite. Faces had changed in the past five years, but their glances were still the same as she passed by. No matter how much she had changed, the fact remained that she was the laird's daughter. Of course, people would notice her. But what struck her as odd was the pitiful looks they gave her. Had someone died? If she was lucky, they mourned Tavish. Aye, but she knew better. Mayhap she should find Neil; he had to know what was going on.

As she searched the great hall, someone gripped her arm from behind. Oh, for the love of saints. She blew out a breath of relief, it had to be her Da.

She turned around. Everything she'd fought so hard to escape and forget was staring her in the face. Her heart raced and she wanted to run away. "Tavish."

He hadn't changed a bit. Still tall and slender with the same smirk. Charm had been his virtue, it allowed him to manipulate people. She knew what evil secrets he held—what kind of man he truly was, vile and selfish.

"'Tis good to see ye sister. Five years is a long time to be away." He smiled and hugged her.

Liar! He was as happy to see her as a thief was happy to see a pillory. His repulsive touch made her sick. "Where's Father?"

Tavish broke their not-so-loving embrace. "Have ye eaten?"

Effie shook her head. Why wouldn't anyone tell her where her father was?

"Here, let's sit and eat." He motioned to a table where a man sat eagerly spooning porridge into his mouth. "I have someone I want ye to meet."

Effie knew the only way to survive was to stay strong. So, she squared her shoulders. She was not the same person she had been five years ago. *Show no fear,* she reminded herself. *No one can hurt you now.*

The man at the table came clearer as they approached. He peered up from his trencher of food and smiled. Aye, how could anyone forget Sir Henry, Baron of Lancaster and the younger brother of Sir Thomas, Earl of Lancaster, one of England's wealthiest and most powerful families? Even though they had never been formally introduced, his reputation was known far and wide.

A fine, English knight, he'd conquered and seized several borderland castles in the name of the late King Edward I.

He stood and bowed. Effie could not miss how tall and handsome he was—short black hair and a perfect smile and white teeth. "Good morn, Mistress Maxwell, 'tis good to make your acquaintance."

"Effie, this is Sir Henry of Lancaster," Tavish introduced.

Effie curtsied. "Good morn."

Sir Henry scooted his trencher over and motioned for Effie to sit. "Join me."

Effie accepted his offer, yet something seemed off. Why was an English knight at Caerlaverock? The north tower was in ruin, no one seemed to want to tell her where her father was, the behavior around her was becoming stranger by the moment.

Tavish sat across from her, giving her a trencher of blood pudding, porridge, and hot fresh bread. She ate everything, but the smell of the food made her feel queasy. Or was it the company she held?

"Will Father be joining us?" she asked.

Tavish bowed his head, and Sir Henry placed his hand on top of hers.

"Tavish, if ye know something, please, I beg ye, tell me," Effie said.

"Effie, there has been an attack on Castle Caerlaverock and on Clan Maxwell. The Douglas's have waged war upon us and tried to seize the north tower. But," he nodded to Sir Henry, "Sir Henry and his garrison came to our aid."

Effie must have looked like a deer about to meet its death. Her heartbeat pounded in her ears. Clan Douglas had attacked her home, but why? It had to be a mistake.

Tavish continued, "Unfortunately, Father was killed by their commander."

Devastated, she covered her mouth to hold back her sobs. Nay, this could not be true! This was the moment when she would wake and everything would go back to normal.

Sir Henry turned to Effie and lightly squeezed her hand. "If it gives you any comfort, we have the man who killed your father in the dungeon."

"Aye," Tavish reassured her, "Most of their men were slaughtered, and those who were not fled back to Angus with their tails tucked."

Effie couldn't believe what she was hearing. Nay, she shook her head, there had to be some kind of misunderstanding. A Douglas would not attack her father. The Maxwells were their allies, and they owed fealty to King Robert. Her father supported the crown with honor.

In order to believe any of this, she had to see the man who had murdered her father.

Effie pulled herself together before speaking. "I want to meet the man who killed father."

∼

The smell of dank earth, urine, and blood assaulted Conall's senses as he began to regain consciousness. His dragon stirred weakly trying to heal himself. By the way his chest ached, he knew he had broken ribs. *Cowards!* Holding a man down to be beaten was not a fair fight. Clan Maxwell had shown their true colors, treacherous bastards!

The foul taste of dirt and iron in his mouth made his stomach lurch. God help those who did this to him. When he got out of there, the whole damn clan would pay, that was certain. Conall curled up on his side as he coughed up blood. "Shite," he groaned.

"About time ye got up."

Conall felt a boot kick his leg.

The mere knowledge that he wasn't alone made Conall pay attention. "Who," he coughed, "are ye and where am I?"

"Ye be in Hell, me friend."

Conall opened his eyes and saw a lad of what he thought to be at least twenty, sitting next to him with his back propped up against the wall.

"Me name is Caden."

Conall sat up holding his side and that's when he noticed the blood seeping through his tunic. He had been stabbed. "How long have I been here?"

"Not as long as some of us. If me guess is right, I'd say two days."

The dungeon was scarcely lit by torches just outside the cell. Enough light to see what kind of shape he was in.

Conall spat up blood, then cleared his throat. "So Caden, why are ye here?"

"Because of who I am."

"And just who be ye?"

As Caden rambled on, Conall shushed him. All of his senses came to life, he could feel Effie's presence, hear and smell her. Conall climbed to his feet and walked to the cell bars, straining to hear her voice. Closing his eyes, he took in a long, deep breath, smelling her sweet honey scent. Aye, Effie was there but why?

She wasn't alone. By all that was mighty if anyone had hurt Effie he would gut them where they stood. The more panicked he became, the more his dragon awakened. He paced the front of the cell as voices drew closer. How did those bastards find her? He swiped a shaking hand through his hair.

The doors to the dungeon opened. If one hair on her pretty little head was out of place...His dragon roared to life, begging to be unleashed. Even weakened, his dragon could raise one hell of a tempestuous storm. If Conall didn't calm down, the dragon would come out.

Tavish was the first to come into view. Then...Thank the gods, Effie was safe; not a scratch as far as he could see. Her green eyes grew wide and she covered her mouth in shock.

"Effie," Conall whispered.

The look on her face was more than he could endure. Her scrutinizing eyes held him with a cold stare.

"'Tis the man that waged his attack on the north tower and killed our father." Tavish pointed to Conall.

Effie stared at him, shaking her head.

"Effie, look at me. Dinnae believe a word he says."

Sir Henry wrapped his arm around Effie's shoulder, consoling her. "I know this must be hard on you, seeing the man who murdered your father."

Effie was silent and kept her eyes fixed on Conall.

Somehow, Conall had to talk to Effie and make her understand that there was no truth in their lies. Since mated Dragonkine could talk to their mates through mind-speak, he prayed it would work. This was his last chance, for he could feel her tension. She was about to break. "Shake yer head if ye can hear me, lass?" He watched her intently, nothing, no response.

"I've seen enough." Effie choked through the shock in her voice, then turned and hastily walked back down the corridor.

"Effie!"

Sir Henry cast Conall a sly grin as he turned to follow her.

"Effie, dinnae leave!" Conall grabbed the bars and quickly let go. Heat torched his skin as if he'd just touched a hot cauldron. "Shite!" He looked down at his reddened hands, as they started to blister. "What's happening?"

Why wasn't he healing? Two days should have been enough time to heal. Blood still oozed from the stab wound, ribs were still broken, and his body showed bruises and cuts. Thankfully he could still feel his dragon, weak, but he was there nonetheless. Nothing made sense.

Tavish slunk up beside him. "I know who ye are. I'm no fool."

"Ye know nothing!"

"Oh, but I do know. Ye see, I have eyes and ears throughout Scotland. I know me sister fancies ye." Tavish leaned in, careful not to get too close. "I know what ye two do in the woods."

Conall stood as close as he could to the bars without touching them. "Effie is yer sister?"

"Aye."

Effie had a brother? For a moment, Conall was taken aback. Effie had never mentioned that she had a brother. *God's wounds! Then that makes Sir Herbert her father.* Tavish's words rang back to him from moments ago, *'Tis the man that waged his attack on the north tower and killed our father. Effie thinks I killed her father.*

Rage like never before boiled inside of him. He had to get to Effie.

"Heed me words well," Conall warned. "If ye lay one finger on Effie, I will kill ye with me own bare hands." It was not said to be a threat but a promise. Conall had never been more serious in his life. He'd failed once at protecting his late wife and son, he would not fail again.

"I do believe ye're in no position to make threats. Ye need no' fash yerself about me sister. I have plans for her." Tavish turned to go.

The impulse to shift was too powerful to hold back. Conall leaned his head back and closed his eyes, waiting for the change. He was going after Effie, she had to know he didn't kill her father. His dragon stirred, but something was wrong.

The dragon grew distressed and began to panic. It shook and rattled with such force, as if it was trying to escape a cage. Conall needed to calm the dragon down, and fast, before they both went insane.

Caden approached Conall. "Let her go. There's no escaping these bars."

In a flash, Conall grabbed Caden by the front of his tunic and unleashed all his pent-up frustrations by ramming the lad's body against the stone wall. Dust and dirt from the ceiling rained down on them from the force.

Conall stared him in the eyes. "What do ye know about these bars?"

Caden smiled. "I know enough to no' touch them."

"Who are ye?" There was something about this whole situation that left a bad taste in Conall's mouth.

7

Finally. Magnus stood to greet James as he entered the solar. The once peaceful Dragonkine elder was having a difficult time staying calm. Being as it was his tenth pint of ale, time seemed to stand still, as he had waited for James a bit longer than he cared to. God's blood, he hadn't just risked his life, escaping the creepers, to turn around and waste more precious time waiting on James. "James, will Rory and Conall be joining us?"

James took a seat behind his desk followed by his two prized Scottish deerhounds, Lennox and Mahboon. "Rory will be here, but Conall had some business to take care of for me."

"I see."

Neither man really wanted to discuss the issues, knowing the future held the possibility of destruction. The earth had been shaking frequently and the force of it all was causing a great concern.

Rory strolled in, nodding at them.

Magnus paced and stroked his beard, thinking of the best way to deliver the news. James sat back in his chair and said, "Och Magnus, ye're making me dizzy. Out with it."

Magnus took a deep breath. "Our worst fears could verra well be upon us." He faced his brethren.

Rory stood by the hearth with his arms folded over his chest. His posture said it all. Every man in the solar was at attention, waiting for Magnus's next words.

"King Drest awakens."

Silence.

"Are ye sure?" James asked.

"Aye, the night Marcus's dragon was taken, King Drest stirred." Magnus detested that he had to be the bearer of bad news. He knew James already hated the fact that he lost control that night and removed Marcus's dragon essence, but it was better than the outcome that could have happened if Magnus hadn't stopped him. Killing Marcus on holy ground would have awakened doom sooner.

Taking Abigale prisoner in order to trap James hadn't sat well with the Kine. Furthermore, Marcus had hidden his dragon. He'd waited for the perfect opportunity to make his move, killing James and spilling his blood on sacred ground had been his plan all along. But what he hadn't counted on was the bond between James and Abigale. No one messed with a dragon's woman and lived to tell the tale. Thank the Gods that Magnus had stopped James in time, before he'd fully killed Marcus.

"I dinnae understand, blood was not shed. I took his dragon, I did no' kill the bastard." James walked to a table in the corner of the room and poured himself a tankard of ale. He drank it down.

"The elders seem to think Marcus is the key to unearthing our past. He will be the one to awaken our king and bring trouble to Scotland. Humans will pay the price for MacAlpin's treachery upon the Kine."

"And what about Dragonkine? Are we to pay the price for the humans' greedy ways?" Rory bit back. It was no secret, Rory wasn't fond of the idea that Dragonkine submitted to human rule.

"I'm afraid it matters no' who ye be, ye're either with them or against them."

"And the death dragons?" James asked.

Magnus shuddered. Anything with the word death attached to it was no good. "The elders would no' say. But I believe they are here to help Marcus bring back King Drest. Do ye remember the part of the tale when seven royals were with King Drest when they fell in the pit of death?"

"Aye."

"These creepers in human form, death dragons are the souls of those men. They are Drest's elite guard. Somehow, they have risen and are helping Marcus. It's the only way I can make any sense of it all."

"This is absurd. Why would Marcus want Drest to awaken? No good can come of this." James began to pace.

"He is our rightful king," Rory added.

James scrubbed a hand down his face. "So, how do we prevail? Abigale is human. I will no' allow any harm to her, me child, or me clan. King Robert has been good to me and Scotland."

"I have a plan, but it may be impossible to execute," Magnus said.

James and Rory stared at Magnus.

"We need to bring all six remaining Dragonkine together. We must build an army to protect Scotland against the attack."

James laughed. "Have ye gone mad? Do ye know what would happen if all of Scotland knew Dragons existed? Humans wouldn't understand. We will be hunted!"

"Abigale accepts ye for who ye are." Magnus dared to bring James's wife into the conversation only because he had to make a point. If the Dragonkine had any hope of victory against Drest, they needed to band together.

James shot Magnus a well-deserved amber glare.

"Even if we were to get humans on our side, how in the bloody hell are we going to bring the Kine together? Do I need to remind ye there's only six of us left, and two of the six are missing? Odds do no' seem to be in our favor," Rory quipped.

The sound of the great hall doors being shoved open echoed up to the solar. James, Magnus, and Rory bolted downstairs. With danger drawing closer, the men were on high alert.

James hit the bottom of the stairs and to his surprise, found Alice tending to a young lad. "Alice?"

"My Laird, 'tis Broc. He's badly wounded." Her hands were soaked in blood.

"Rory, fetch me wife. Magnus, help bring the lad upstairs to an empty bedchamber," James ordered.

"There's one available on your right," Alice said as she hurried to the kitchen to prepare some hot water.

No sooner had the men laid Broc down on the bed, Abigale and Rory walked in to the bedchamber.

"Abigale, Broc needs your attention," James said.

Abigale looked at her husband, then to the lad. "Do we know what happened?" Abigale ripped Broc's blood-stained tunic open.

Alice rushed in with boiling water and cloth.

The lad moaned in pain and tried to talk. "Maxwell... Conall."

James bent down by Broc's head. "What happened?"

Broc fought hard in between labored breaths. "It was a trap." He swallowed hard as Abigale wiped a wet cloth over his forehead.

"Maxwell's men attacked us." The pain was too much to bear and the lad slipped into unconsciousness.

James stepped out of the bedchamber, in shock. Magnus and Rory followed.

"Conall is in danger. I can feel it," James said. "I must go to his aid."

"Nay, James. Your wife is with child, ye stay here and me and Rory will go," Magnus said.

"Aye, I can find him and be back before Abigale goes into labor." Rory winked.

"Nay, I will go!" James said through gritted teeth. "Conall's me best friend and I put him in danger."

Abigale walked out of the bedchamber wiping the blood from her hands on a cloth. "Go where?"

James raked his hand through his hair. "How's Broc?"

"He's been stabbed. The wound looks as if it happened a couple of days ago. 'Tis no' deep. And he's been badly beaten. Alice is cleaning the lad's cuts as we speak."

James was silent.

"Do ye plan to tell me where the three of ye be going?" Abigale looked at each of them.

James didn't want to worry Abigale, nor place his burden on her, yet he knew his wife well. In no matter would she allow him to leave Angus without telling her what was going on and where he was headed.

"Conall could be in some trouble. I need to go to Caerlaverock Castle and make sure he's all right."

"Clan Maxwell?"

"Aye."

"Effie left a day ago to visit her father at Caerlaverock Castle," Alice blurted as she came out of the bedchamber.

"Effie's a Maxwell?" James's brows furrowed in question.

Alice fidgeted with her apron. "Please forgive me, laird. I promised no' to tell."

"Do ye think they are both in some kind of trouble?" Abigale asked.

James rubbed his hands over Abigale's shoulders. "Dinnae worry, love. 'Tis no' good for the babe."

"Aye," Rory agreed. "Three dragons can defeat one clan without any problem. We'll be back before the evening meal."

Abigale smiled at Rory's jest. "Ye must be back soon." She rubbed her belly. "And bring back Effie."

James kissed his wife with so much passion and love he thought his heart would burst. He felt her distress, for he understood. Both of their friends were in danger. By the condition that Broc was in, Conall had to be worse off.

James broke their kiss and whispered softly, "I love ye."

Abigale took his head in her hands and gently rubbed her thumbs over his whiskered jawline. "Go find our friends and come back to me."

"Magnus, ye'll stay here. I need a dragon to protect the castle."

"Aye."

"I want at least ten heavily armed guards with Abigale at all times."

Abigale shot James an aggravated look.

"Och lass, five then. Five guards and I will no' have any less."

Abigale smiled at her husband's overprotectiveness.

James began to make his way to the stables. "Oh, and Magnus, the gates are to stay closed until our return."

"Aye."

Funny how love could change a man. He never wanted a wife before he met Abigale, nor did he want to play the part of a clan chief, yet here he was and he had never felt more content and alive in his life. This is who he was born to be, a mated Dragonkine warrior protecting his family.

~

Marcus rolled onto his back as he sucked in the frigid air. As he moved, he heard crunching beneath him as if he was lying on top of a blanket of snow. *Snow?* he thought. The last thing he remembered was falling from his horse and seeing a trail of blood in the snow. Was he still in the forest?

Wind howled around him. Where was he? The sound of dripping water echoed through his head.

With great effort, he opened his eyes and soon realized that he was in a cave, a dark icy cave. Struggling to a sitting position, he searched the space for any signs of life. Marcus tried to call out but it was difficult to speak.

An empty feeling tore at his chest. He was missing a part of himself, his dragon. All of his life he had searched for inner peace, trying to accept who he was. He'd cursed the day he transformed into Dragonkine. The more he'd fought it, the stronger his dragon grew.

Being around his cousin, James Douglas, hadn't helped. James accepted his dragon and it had blessed him with power and skills as a warrior. Marcus, on the other hand, had kept his dragon a secret. His dragon had never begged to reveal itself, instead, it kept quiet. Marcus envied his cousin and had grown as cold as his dragon.

Now that his dragon was gone, he yearned to feel him again.

Marcus stood. He shuffled his way to the mouth of the cave and stopped and looked over the edge. Blue-gray skies filled his view. The distant call of a hawk sounded over the mountaintops. The ice cave was in the highest peak in the Highlands. But how did he get there?

Tired and in agonizing pain, he required more sleep to heal. Like any human, he was weak. He returned to his resting spot, tunneling into the snow to keep warm. Somehow, the cold comforted his restless soul. There'd be plenty of time to figure out what he needed to do next. He yawned and closed his eyes, hoping his lost dragon would fill his dreams.

8

*E*ffie had made it back to her bedchamber just in time to vomit in an empty pitcher sitting next to her nightstand. Maggie rushed to her side and held her hair. When Effie looked at the maid, Maggie noticed the tears in her eyes and gave her a sympathetic look

"Here, come sit down." She motioned for Effie to sit on the bed, then went to the table and grabbed a cloth and some water.

This all had to be a nightmare. Conall locked in a dungeon, accused of murder. Seeing him had broken her heart but hearing his desperate cry for help...It had nearly destroyed her. Why would he attack her home? *It could not be true.*

"Here mistress, take this." Maggie handed Effie a wet cloth "Is there anything I can do for ye?"

Effie shook her head. There was nothing anyone could do to ease the pain inside her heart.

Emotionally drained, Effie laid down on the bed. Why was this happening to her? Why was fate being so cruel again? With her father dead, no one was there to protect her. It wouldn't be long before Tavish would make demands again. Effie sobbed into her pillow.

She should have known better than to run from her past. No matter how far you got, the past always caught up in the end.

Maggie tucked the fur around Effie. "I'll leave ye to rest." As she stepped away, Effie grabbed her wrist.

"Please, stay. I dinnae want to be alone." Effie scooted over. "Please." Maggie slipped her shoes off and crawled into bed. Effie stretched out next to her. "When I was a wee girl, me mum used to cuddle with me when I was sick."

"Aye, mistress— "

"Call me Effie."

"Aye. There's nothing like a mother's love when ye're sick."

"Are ye close with yer mum?" Effie asked.

"Aye, I visit her when I get a break."

Effie smiled, remembering the stories her mum would tell about mischievous fairies that turned mean ladies into frogs with warts. She would do anything to have her mother with her right now.

"Me mum died when I was young," Effie confessed.

"Me deepest apologies." Maggie stroked Effie's hair.

"'Twas a sad day for all of us. She was beautiful and proud." Effie smiled sadly. "I remember a time when I came home filthy from doing chores. I was so mad at her for making me help the stable lads clean stalls. I stomped up to me room to find me mum waiting for me. She was sad. Me da had betrayed her but she wouldn't say what had happened."

Maggie fell silent, allowing Effie to reminisce.

"Have ye ever been betrayed before...by someone ye loved?"

Maggie grew quiet.

"'Tis okay. Ye dinnae have to tell me."

Maggie rolled over on her side, facing Effie. "I have," she sighed. "'Tis something I dinnae talk about. However, I have learned that sometimes the person who ye think has betrayed ye really hasn't."

Effie paused for a moment, taking in Maggie's words. Did Conall really betray her or had it been her brother? Aye, the events that had taken place over the last few days left many questions unanswered. Still having a difficult time believing that Laird Douglas would order an attack against an allied clan, Effie needed proof. In addition, her heart still wasn't ready to accept the fact that Conall was a murderer.

After her stomach settled, she sat up. "Maggie, do ye know much about the attack on the north tower?"

"Nay, I was visiting me mum when it happened. When I returned, Tavish had held a gathering after the attack blaming Clan Douglas. Sir Henry and his garrison came to our aid."

"Why would the English help us, knowing me father supports King Robert?" She slipped her feet into her shoes.

Maggie shrugged. "I'm sorry, but I dinnae know."

Something was terribly amiss. She needed to find Neil. "Please excuse me, Maggie. I must leave."

"Aye, I must be getting back to work meself." Maggie smiled.

Effie washed her face, then looked at her maid. "Thank ye for being me friend."

Maggie nodded shyly as she left the chamber.

Effie made her way to her father's solar. 'Twas the one place where she could feel close to him. To her surprise, the door was unlocked. She peeked inside.

Her father's desk still stood in the same place, just like she remembered. When she was a child, she would sit on her da's lap while he worked signing charters, reviewing figures, and settling disputes within the clan. Here is where he'd taught her how to read and the responsibilities of being a laird. Those had been some of the happiest moments of her life.

Even after a long day, Sir Herbert always made time for her.

A massive bookcase stood on one side of the solar and on the other, a hearth where her father's sword and leather targe hung. The sunlight from the small window reflected off her father's sword as Effie walked closer to admire the pair.

Her father was a great warrior. Now that he was gone, who would take his place? Who could possibly lead Clan Maxwell as proudly and honorably as her father?

Voices from outside brought Effie's attention to the door. She walked to the door and listened. Two men were talking, but she couldn't make out the words. As she listened, her body stiffened as one of the voices came clear. *Tavish.* His sinister voice sent a chill down her spine.

As their footsteps grew closer, she didn't have time to escape before her brother entered. She had to hide. Quickly, she scurried behind the desk and hoped the men didn't find her.

"Me sister looked verra bonny this morn, what say ye?" Tavish swelled with pride as he and Sir Henry made their way into the solar.

"Indeed, Tavish."

Tavish walked over to the desk and poured two drams of whiskey.

"However, I do not fully trust ye."

Tavish handed Henry a dram. "Now that I'm the laird, I can assure ye there's nothing to worry about. Ye have gained an ally."

Henry eyed Tavish with suspicion as he drank the whiskey. "Your plan had better work."

"Aye, I have me sister under control."

"Need I remind you of our agreement? I've ceased my attack on the north tower and allowed your filthy Scotsmen to stay here at Caerlaverock." Sir Henry paused. "A fool I must be. You know what I want in return for the mercy I've shown your people."

Tavish placed a firm hand on Henry's shoulder. "Nay, my lord, I need no reminding. Rest assured, ye will receive yer wish."

Henry grimaced as he stared at Tavish's hand on his shoulder and shrugged it off. "I'm not keen on marrying a Scotswoman. They are more trouble than they are worth."

"No' Effie. She'll be an obedient wife. And ye have me word, Clan Maxwell will be loyal to the English crown."

"Marriage? To an English knight?" Effie raised her head, banging it on the desk. *Oh, for the love of saints!* She held back a cry. How could she have been so careless?

Effie watched Tavish's boots draw near. Panic-stricken, she realized he heard her. She had to come up with a plan and fast, for if her brother caught her, he would beat her senseless. Looking down at her clenched hands, she felt the ring Conall had given her.

She removed the ring and gathered all the confidence she could muster before she made her presence known. Facing Tavish was like meeting the devil himself.

"Och, there ye are," Effie announced and stood up from under the desk with the ring in her hand. "Oh!" she cried out in shock as she looked at Tavish and then to Sir Henry. "What are ye up to sneaking up on a lass like that?" With a surprised look on her face, she placed her hand on her chest as if she was startled. "I thought to be alone."

"Please pardon our intrusion, mistress," Sir Henry said.

"What are ye doing in here, Effie?"

"I wanted to find a book to read and me ring slipped off and rolled under the desk. I am lucky to have found it." Effie was playing her part well and thought just maybe she would escape this situation without a beating.

"Aye, I see. Well, since ye're here, we have some business to attend to." Tavish looked over at Henry.

By the way the two men glanced at each other, Effie knew they were up to no good. "I'll leave ye to yer business. 'Tis nice to see ye again, Sir Henry." Effie grabbed a book and began to make her exit when Tavish stopped her.

"Don't leave quite yet, Sister. This business concerns ye."

Tavish paced in front of the hearth with his hands folded behind his back. "Dear sister, once our father is laid to rest, I will be appointed clan chief. And as chief, me first duty is to arrange yer betrothal."

Effie took a step back.

"I believe it would suit clan Maxwell verra well to be in good favor with King Edward. Ye will marry Sir Henry of Lancaster to ensure our loyalty to England."

Before she could stop herself, she blurted, "Nay, I will no' do it."

Tavish advanced on Effie so quickly she didn't have time to think. His hands wrapped around her throat and squeezed. "Are ye defying me orders?"

Effie shook her head, for she couldn't speak.

"I know all about yer dragon down in the dungeon," he seethed. "He will be found guilty of murder and will be punished for his crime. Do ye understand me?"

Effie frantically grabbed at his hands trying to free herself.

"Ye will do as I say or yer precious dragon will suffer the same fate as William." Tavish stared deep into her eyes, confirming what she'd feared, he had murdered William. Effie's body grew weightless the harder her brother squeezed her throat.

"If ye want me to show yer dragon mercy ye'll do what I say."

Henry strode up to Tavish and shoved him off Effie. She fell to the floor, gasping for air.

Henry grabbed Tavish by the front of his tunic and shoved him up against the wall. "A true man shouldn't have to lay his hand upon a woman. Heed my words, do not touch your sister again. She's mine now and I will not have her damaged." The cold stare from Henry was enough to make any man wet himself.

Henry pushed Tavish toward the door. Tavish smoothed his plaid and then retreated from the solar but couldn't resist one last scowl in Effie's direction.

Sir Henry bent down in front of Effie. "He won't touch you again, I assure you."

Still gasping for air, Effie placed her hand on her throat and looked up into the knight's light brown eyes. "Thank ye."

Sir Henry helped her up. "We shall marry soon. I have some business to take care of and then we will go to Northumberland."

Her throat burned but she couldn't stay silent. "I... will no' go, nor marry ye."

Henry chuckled. He gazed at her. "Mistress, you'll find I'm a tolerant man, for the most part." He stroked her cheek with his thumb. "But I must warn you, when I set my eyes on something I want," he looked her up and down, "I will not be denied."

Effie swallowed hard. He most definitely was a powerful knight, and it would benefit her greatly to obey his orders. Yet this was her life and she would not be told who to marry.

"Yer an English high-born, why would ye want to marry a Scottish lass?"

"I have seized many castles across Scotland, yet no matter how many I hold, the desire for more consumes me." Henry strode back to the corner table and poured himself another dram. "It's not until now that I have realized that it's not the castles, nor the riches that I desire. I desire to conquer a Scottish lass."

Effie's brows furrowed in disbelief. Had she heard him correctly? She was no more than a conquest to him?

"Now, I suggest you get some rest and join me for the evening meal." Henry escorted her out of the solar and to her bedchamber.

Once safely in her room, she realized that in less than two days, she had found out her father had been murdered by the man she loved and now she was to wed an English knight and leave Scotland. Could things get any worse?

9

The great hall of clan Maxwell was filled with several hundred clansmen partaking of the night's feast of lamb, fish, and an array of vegetables. Sir Henry and his captains sat at the head table. The gathering of Clan Maxwell and the English had begun.

Sitting directly across from Effie, her brother gloated. A sly grin spread across his face as he nodded and raised his tankard to her. Effie cringed. The sight of him made her stomach turn.

Feeling constricted by the ribbon tied around her neck, she tried to loosen it and still keep the bruises concealed. It had been a difficult task for Maggie and her to find a wide enough ribbon to hide the marks on her neck. She wore her hair down, which helped, too.

The evening meal had been served, and Effie merely picked at it. Not pleased to be betrothed to Sir Henry, she moved the carrots around on her trencher. She'd spent the night trying to figure out how she was going to get herself out of this mess. Running away had been a short-lived plan. With the power that Henry and now her brother held, she would have been caught in no time. But she had to do something. Knowing now Conall had nothing to do with the attack, it terrified her what Tavish was doing.

Still, Alice had promised to send help if she didn't return.

Effie huffed in defeat as her eyes stayed focused down on the escaping vegetable. The longer she stayed here the more she could feel herself slipping back into that scared defenseless little girl she'd been years ago. This place most definitely was destined to be the cause of her death if she didn't do something to change her fate.

"'Tis rude to pick at your food," Sir Henry said as he wiped his mouth on a linen cloth.

Apparently, her table manners were not to his liking, but she didn't care. She met his scrutinizing glare. "Please forgive me, my laird." She bit into the carrot spitefully.

Leaning in so only she could hear him he said, "I like a spirited woman." He slipped his hand under the table and placed it on Effie's thigh. "I will only warn you once, when we're in public, you will be a proper wife. Do you understand me?" He squeezed her leg. "For you will not like my choice in punishment for disobedience." He kissed her softly on the cheek.

Henry's grip tightened and his nails dug into her thigh. "I beg you not test my patience."

Something snapped inside her. She grabbed his hand and pushed it off of her. Without causing a scene, she said. "Intimidation will no' make me an obedient wife." She grabbed his ballocks. "Threaten me again, and these become a trophy for me to hang on me wall."

Henry swallowed hard and was about to say something when Tavish stood and called everyone to attention. "As ye all know by now, Sir Herbert Maxwell, me father, has entered through Heaven's gates. May he rest in peace."

A large part of the crowd repeated his words. "Rest in peace."

Tavish continued. "As his only son, I have inherited the seat as chief of Clan Maxwell. Once the charter has been signed, I will be yer leader."

The great hall stood silent. Effie looked around the hall, no one seemed happy about this announcement. Not the warm welcome Tavish had wanted.

A man stood up at the back of the hall. "What will be done to the men who attacked our tower and murdered our chief? I believe I speak on behalf of all clansmen. Justice should be served."

"No one wants justice as much as I do," Tavish lied. "The man who murdered me father is in the dungeon and awaits punishment."

"But why wait? Let the bastard pay." The room erupted with applause.

Tavish glanced at Sir Henry. "So, the clan has spoken, aye?" A symphony of ayes echoed. "A public flogging, aye?"

The man turned behind him as if asking the clan mockingly. "Flogging?" The crowd grumbled. "Nay." He stood firm and crossed his arms over his chest.

"Trial by combat!" Tavish yelled as he held his goblet high and the room exploded with the Maxwell war cry.

There was nothing worthier of approval to the Highlanders as announcing a bloody brawl. They were bred to fight to the death.

Tavish quieted the room. "To ensure further protection, I'm pleased to announce that me sister, Effie, will marry Sir Henry of Lancaster, joining our great houses under English rule."

The celebration ceased.

"I know this is a sudden change. But our brothers to the north have betrayed us. Sir Henry has assured us protection."

Sir Henry stood. "To show my word is true, it shall be my honor to fight the accused. I will avenge my betrothed's father." He looked down at Effie and smiled.

She couldn't believe what she was hearing. Torn between seeking justice for her father and believing that the man she loved hadn't killed him, she didn't know what to do. If Conall had killed her father, he still deserved a fair trial. This was not justice.

As the crowd cheered over drams of whiskey, Effie excused herself and made her way to Tavish. She had to talk some sense into him. "Tavish, may I have a word with ye?"

"Oh, aye, what be on yer mind?" His false kindness made her stomach turn.

"Ye must grant a trial to the accused."

Tavish's glared at her. "Dinnae ye want the man who killed Father to pay for what he has done to our family?"

"If he's guilty."

Tavish latched onto her arm and pulled her close. "I be the chief now. Dinnae ever question me command. Yer dragon will pay for what he has done." Tavish pushed her aside and walked away.

Effie stood speechless. She wasn't excepting him to be cordial to her, but she didn't except to be ignored either. He was already consumed by power. As she looked over the hall, watching her brother greet and talk with fellow clansmen, she could see a shift in Clan Maxwell. They now welcomed the idea of being under English control. Something that would have never happened if her father was still alive. Shame on her brother.

Effie stormed out of the hall. She strode through the courtyard, over the bridge until she found herself standing next to her parents' graves under the auld rowan tree.

Effie fell to her knees and cried. She grabbed a clump of dirt from atop her father's freshly filled grave and threw it as far as she could, angry and overwhelmed with sorrow. They left her with Tavish. They left her alone.

She sat back on her heels. What she wouldn't give to have them back. She tried to be the daughter they would be proud of. That's why she had never told her da about Tavish and what he'd made her do. She had always been her da's wee lass.

Needing to be close to her parents, she crawled between their graves and rested her cheek on the cold stone marking her father's mound. Pulling her cloak tighter around her body, she said, "Da, please forgive me for leaving the way I did. I wish I could have stayed."

"Och, lass, yer da was verra proud of ye."

Effie looked up. "Neil!" Effie cried as she shot up and raced toward the Highlander. Finally, a familiar face. Wrapping her arms around him, she wept freely. "Thank God ye're here."

"Sweet lass, I'm sorry about yer father. I should have told ye sooner." Neil folded his arms around her.

"Tis no fair."

"I know. Yer father was a good man. He left us too early." Neil looked down at the graves.

"Tavish is out of control. He's going to kill the man in the dungeon for murdering father. He deserves a fair trial, no?"

"Effie, that man did no' kill yer father."

Effie took a step back, confused as to what she had just heard. "What do ye mean?"

"Sir Henry attacked the north tower. Tavish convinced everyone that Clan Douglas was behind the attack and those of us who asked questions…well."

Effie understood what he was saying. No commander as loyal as Neil would surrender to a tyrant, unless the consequences were deadly to his men-at-arms.

"I knew something wasn't right."

"Aye."

"Oh, dear God!" Effie covered her mouth. How could she have doubted Conall's honor?

Neil looked at Effie. "Do ye know that man?"

"Aye."

"Lass, he was here to discuss some business with yer father. But when he arrived, yer da had already passed on."

"But he sent me a message, or at least I thought it was him." Effie began to pace in deep thought.

"Yer father had been ill but the healer had said he was showing signs of recovery. Besides, yer father dinnae know where ye were. He could no' have sent ye a message."

"Tavish must have sent it."

"I wouldn't put it past the swine."

"But why? Why does he want me here?" Effie pondered some more. She didn't need to be there in order for him to inherit her father's title. Unless she was there for something else Tavish was planning. "Henry."

"Aye, I'm truly sorry for that arrangement, lass."

"Henry attacked the tower, aye?"

"Aye."

"So, the attack happened before Conall arrived."

"Aye."

"Tavish wanted the attack to look like Laird Douglas provoked it. Knowing Conall was on his way here, it was the perfect opportunity to blame the attack and murder on Conall. I'm here to keep the peace with the English."

"Lass, why would Tavish go to such lengths just to become chief. It was his by birthright."

"I overheard Tavish and Henry talking about an agreement between the two of them. I bet he made a truce with Henry to stop the attack on the tower."

"I have eyes and ears everywhere. I would have known about Tavish's scheme."

"Nay, Neil. Ye dinnae understand. Tavish will stop at nothing to get what he wants. Think about it. The attack was set up to look like Conall and his men did it and Henry stopped it, gaining our loyalty. While this was happening, Tavish killed Father. Now he has the authority to marry me to Henry."

"Neil, do ye think Tavish murdered Father?"

He looked around before he answered. "Aye, I do."

"We have to do something about it. An innocent man can no' be punished for a crime he didnae commit."

She wouldn't let Tavish harm her beloved. "I need to see the prisoner. Can ye help me?"

Neil nodded.

"Thank ye." She embraced him again, knowing she owed him so much for his unwavering loyalty to her father. "I want to see him now."

"Tis not the right time." Neil stopped her. "His cell is well guarded. I'll come for ye later. But first, I must give ye this." Neil reached into his jerkin and handed her a missive. "Yer father wanted ye to have it."

Effie looked at the scroll and back to Neil as if she was afraid to touch it. *Father's last words.* Her heart sank and her chest tightened. She wasn't ready to read it.

"Lass, I'll find ye tonight. Until then, stay in your bedchamber."

She had to find a way to free Conall. She was the reason he was in this predicament. If she would have stood up to her evil brother all those years ago, her father might still be alive.

Wiping a tear from her cheek, she squared her shoulders and made her way to her bedchamber. She'd be damned if she lost both men she loved to Tavish. He would pay for his endless sins, that much she knew.

Effie quickly opened her bedchamber door and stepped inside. She laid the missive on her table, then took a step back. She stared at the parchment. Her father's last words to her. Aye, she was curious to read it but couldn't. What if he hadn't forgiven her? What if this missive was nothing more than her father disowning her.

Effie sighed and walked away.

She washed her face and hands. As she patted her face dry, she eyed her harp in the corner. It had been years since she played. Effie walked over and sat behind the instrument. She smiled and closed her eyes as she strummed the strings. She would play a beloved tune for her da.

10

*T*ime would always be the bane of his existence. Unlike humans, his existence had no starting point or ending. But one thing held true, a Dragonkine without his mate was an untamed beast.

As Conall sat reflecting, he could feel his dragon rattling about, hungry for bloodshed. He desperately needed to get out of there fast.

His only meal, more like slop, was sticky porridge and stale bread. Conall broke off a piece and popped it in his mouth. He eyed the iron bars of his cell. His suspicion was right, they were laced with magic to keep him inside and his dragon dormant. In fact, the entire cell had been enchanted, he could feel it all around him, pulsing with dark energy. His wounds had not healed, he was weak, and his dragon was locked up tighter than a virgin before her wedding night. Someone had gone to great lengths to ensure his captivity.

A rat scurried across the dirty floor and over to Conall's porridge bowl. He grabbed a small rock and threw it at the critter, hitting it. It let out a high-pitched squeal and scampered off. "Bloody rats," Conall hissed.

"Looks to me ye found yerself a friend," Caden jested.

"Bugger off, ye lout. I'm in no mood for yer jesting." Conall popped another piece of bread in his mouth.

"Och, lout? That's the pot calling the cauldron black." Caden obviously had no boundaries when it came to his mouth. Just like a young lad, he was full of himself.

The rat came back for more. This time, Conall let the damn thing eat his porridge.

"That thing sure has some bollocks," Caden said.

Conall leaned against the wall for support. The fight inside him was diminishing.

"Ye dinnae look good." Caden squatted in front of Conall. "Ye're pale. Dinnae tell me yer giving up on that lass."

"'Tis no concern of yers," Conall croaked, swallowing hard. "Let me be."

Caden shook his head. "I'll see if I can fetch ye some water." He stood and walked over to the bars without touching them. "Guard!" he called. "We need water!"

As if he had fallen into some kind of state between consciousness and a dream, Conall swore he heard the faint sound of harp music. He had to be mistaken, yet his hearing did not deceive him. There it was again, the softly played notes soothing his body.

Conall closed his eyes and took in the enchanting music. It calmed the whirlwind storm brewing inside to a peaceful standstill. Even his dragon purred in bliss.

Just when he thought he would give up, there was an overwhelming call for survival from deep within his soul, pulling him closer to Effie. She was the center of his universe, life would not be worth living without her. A slight smile crept across his face as he listened to the music, just like that bloody rat that never gave up until it got what it wanted, Conall vowed to fight until his last breath for his Effie.

He must have dozed off, for the grinding moan of the dungeon's doors startled him. He was waiting to hear the heavy footfalls of the guards as their weapons clanged together, but it was silent, as though whoever had entered didn't want to be heard.

And then there it was, sweeping over his body like a cool breeze scented with the smell of sweet honey, awakening him. Her smell was intoxicating.

Effie came into sight, and Conall stood slowly, brushing the dust off his kilt. He must look like death as he ran his fingers through his dirty hair. He was filthy and unshaven.

As he got closer to her, he didn't know what she was thinking. Did she believe the lies Tavish had told her? Furthermore, did she think him capable of murder? *Of course she knows I'm capable. I am a dragon.* He reached the bars but treaded softly, unsure of how Effie would react to him.

Effie nervously approached the cell. "I'm sorry, I should have told ye about me past."

"Why didnae ye tell me ye were a Maxwell?"

"I was ashamed, no' of me name but of me past. Conall, Tavish did awful things to me. He blackmailed me." She looked down at her hands. "There were times I wanted to tell ye, but I...I just couldn't."

"Effie, 'tis no' yer fault. I love ye no matter what." Conall slipped his arm through the bars and caressed her face.

"Even if I was forced to be a whore?"

Conall paused, his jaw tightened. He kept his composure in front of Effie, yet he raged inside and begged to wrap his hands around the bastard's neck. "Effie, look at me."

She gazed into his eyes.

"'Tis no' yer fault. Yer brother will pay heavily for what he has done to ye. Ye are not the same lass as ye were back then."

She shook her head.

"Ye're hurt." Effie pointed at the bloodstain on his tunic.

Conall looked down. "Aye, ye should see the other man." He cocked a brow and grinned.

"I'm sorry, I should have come to ye sooner. Are ye hurting?"

"Nay, I'm fine. What about ye? Are ye well?"

Tears welled in her eyes as she looked up at Conall.

"Och, lass, dinnae cry. I'll find a way to get us out of here." Conall wiped her tears away.

"'Tis no' possible, Conall. Me brother has accused ye of murder and is no' going to give ye a fair trial. A trial by combat has been issued as punishment."

"I do no' care about a trial. I need to know, Effie, do ye believe I killed yer father?"

"Nay, I know ye're innocent. 'Tis all Tavish's doing to bring me back home. I'm so sorry."

Conall's jaw ticked again when he heard the bastard's name.

"Conall, yer wound is still bleeding and it looks deep."

Alas, he couldn't hide the fact that he had been stabbed. His tunic had been sliced and was now stained with blood.

"And ye dinnae look good."

"Och, lass, I am in a dungeon."

"Stop jesting. I'm serious." Effie looked down the corridor. Neil had taken care of the guards for at least the night. No man, even a Sassenach, could turn down a few drams of fine Scottish whiskey. The guards would be piss-drunk long into the next morn.

Fishing a key from her basket, Effie began to unlock the cell. "I'm going to get ye out of here."

Had she gone mad? He was a prisoner, surely she knew if she released him they both had to escape together, which would not be easy. He had no plan, no weapons, and he was too weak to shift.

"What are ye doing? If ye're going to release me, then we go together. I won't allow ye to stay and take the punishment for me escape."

Effie paused before opening the door. "Conall, ye must shift and leave this Godforsaken place. Tavish won't stop until I've suffered enough and ye're dead!"

"Lass, I can no' shift, I'm too weak."

"Och, then we'll have to heal ye."

Conall didn't think he could ever love another woman more than he loved Effie right now. The moment her freckled face and red, curly hair came into view, his body had instantly reacted. He ached for her touch; his dragon purred in contentment just from the sound of her voice.

If he wasn't covered in blood and dirt, as soon as she opened the damn door, he would take her right there. Pin her up against the stone wall, slide her dress over the curve of her hips, and slide into her womanhood until he felt the bittersweet sting of her nails across his back. Then he would do it all over again.

The lock clicked, and Effie swung the door open but quickly halted when a shadow appeared from the corner of the cell.

Conall faced his cellmate. Without speaking, he flashed his reptilian eyes at Caden, daring him to challenge his escape.

Caden nodded and retreated into the shadows.

"Who is that?" Effie asked with wide eyes.

"That's Caden," Conall said. "Dinnae fash yerself over him. He'll behave."

Until Conall stepped out of the cell, he hadn't realized how much he'd missed his freedom. While Effie locked the door, he stood behind her and inhaled the scent of her hair. By the saints, he needed her.

Conall pinned her against the wall and took her face in his hands. "Thank ye, lass." For a moment time stood still; the dungeon melted away, the moaning sounds of prisoners were muted, and all that mattered was the two of them. Perhaps immortality wasn't so bad after all, for he could spend eternity staring into her forest-green eyes.

Effie broke their trance as she reached for a fire torch. "We dinnae have much time. Follow me."

Walking briskly down the corridor and passing several occupied cells, she rounded the corner to a dead-end. What looked to be a regular wall revealed a secret door as soon as Effie placed the key into a hidden keyhole.

"Damn door! Open!" Effie cursed as she tried to force it open.

"Here, let me try." Effie stepped aside, giving Conall enough room to slide in. With one shove, the door creaked open.

A secret passageway was revealed by the torchlight, and it snaked in multiple directions. "Effie, what are you up to?"

"This castle has a lot of secrets, Conall, and this one happens to be mine."

About fifty paces down the main passageway, a ladder came into view. Once up the ladder, another shorter corridor was revealed, then another door. This entrance lead to a secret room. "I used to come here to escape Tavish," she explained. "This is where I would dream of meeting me Highlander."

"Yer Highlander?" he repeated.

"Aye." Her soft gaze warmed him from the inside out.

Conall shut the door as Effie lit a fire in the hearth. The room was quaint. A wooden tub sat in front of the hearth, large enough for him. Effie had already started heating water for a bath. A large poster bed with pillows and furs awaited them, too. His cock hardened as he thought about Effie naked and lying on that bed waiting for him.

Suddenly an apple was shoved at his chest. "Eat this while I fetch a chair." Effie gave him an I-know-what-you're-thinking smile.

～

Effie placed the chair next to the tub. With fire burning in her dragon's eyes, she'd be lucky to get his wounds wrapped before he had his way with her. She yearned to touch him, to feel his weight on top of her again. The best way to speed up his healing process was to stir the dragon.

Effie dipped her hand in the water. It was perfectly warm. Flicking the water off her hand at Conall, she demanded, "Clothes off, Dragon."

Conall stripped off his tunic and shoes. "As ye wish." He winked. "Though in me weakened state, I will need some assistance removing me plaid. The pin is quite tricky."

Effie rolled her eyes. As she approached him, she could feel the heat radiating from his body. Effie didn't dare look him in the eyes as she focused on the material wrapped around his waist. As she finished removing his tartan, she stepped out of his reach and took his dirty clothes to a wash bin to soak.

Hisses of pain brought her attention back to Conall as he slowly submerged himself in the water. Her heart dropped. She wished she could take his pain away. Effie hurried out of her dress, not wanting to get it wet, but left her shift on. After she'd pinned her hair up, she grabbed some soap and sat down in the chair next to the tub.

Taking a small cup, she dipped it into the water and wet his hair. Next, she lathered the soap in her hands. Threading her fingers through his dark brown hair, she noticed it had grown; it now curled just below his ears. Conall leaned his head back, almost reaching her lap, and closed his eyes, moaning as she gently massaged his head. It pleased her to know she was easing his pain.

When she was done with his hair her curiosity got the best of her. Conall had never had facial hair before, and she wanted to touch it. Effie slid her hands from his hair down to his cheeks until she reached his chin. The coarseness of whiskers sent a chill down her spine.

"Ye like the beard, aye?" Conall asked.

"'Tis different on ye," she said, trying to hide her arousal. "Sit up. I need to wash yer back."

She rubbed a cloth across his broad shoulders and up his neck, taking in the raw beauty of this man. She bit her lip as she stroked his strong arms to his chest. Every inch of him fascinated her, so much that she dropped the cloth right into his lap.

"Och lass, looks like ye dropped something." Conall looked down. "Ye'll have to come in and get it."

Her body tingled just thinking about the delicious possibilities her dragon, could bring her.

"Well, I see ye give me no choice." Effie stood. The glow from the hearth illuminated her shift and left nothing to the imagination. "But the shift stays on," she teased.

"As ye wish."

Effie knew exactly what she was doing as she lowered herself into the tub. Steam rolled off her body. As much as she wanted him, he needed to play nice until she could tend to his wounds, especially the one right below his right rib. But there were so many wounds that weren't healing and it worried her. "Conall?"

"Hmm," he said

"Me cloth." Effie held out her hand.

With one fluid motion, Conall swept his arm around Effie's waist and pulled her closer so she had to straddle him. "Yer cloth, mistress."

She snatched it from his hand and then started to wash his chest and cleanse his wounds.

As she cleaned away the grime and blood, he kissed her forehead ever so gently. That's when she knew she liked the beard. He continued kissing down the side of her face and to her neck. Of course, he wouldn't make this easy on her. She craved his touch as much as he craved hers.

"Conall?"

He nuzzled into her neck, purring.

"Why are ye no' healing?" She pulled back to look at him. She needed to know why because if he was going to be battling for his life he needed to heal. For the love of saints, why didn't the man just shift and escape this hell?

Conall raised his hands and showed her his blistered palms. "Someone has cast binding magic so I wouldn't escape. I grabbed the bars the day ye first came to see me and this is what happened."

She examined his hands, shocked at what she found, burns.

"And I can no' shift either. 'Tis like he's trapped inside me, weak and furious. From the moment we arrived, I felt something was amiss here." Conall blew out a breath in frustration.

Effie shook her head. "How would Tavish know that ye're Dragonkine? And he doesn't know magic. At least not that I know of."

"Tavish is up to something but I dinnae know what." Conall shrugged.

Carefully, she continued to clean the stab wound. Effie wondered the same thing; just what was her brother up to? Throughout her life she had known him to be a self-centered, manipulating bastard. Power and greed pumped through his veins with a force that drove him to do unspeakable deeds. Whoring her out was just one of many sins—why not murder, too?

"I know." Effie looked up to meet Conall's gaze. "He's now chief of Clan Maxwell. He accused ye and clan Douglas of the attack on the north tower."

"Effie, the tower was in ruins when we arrived. I came here on business, not to destroy yer home. I was shocked when ye came to see me in the dungeon. I never knew ye're a Maxwell. Ye do believe me?"

Effie nodded. "Aye. I found it hard to believe that laird James would attack me clan."

Conall rubbed his hands up and down her arms, comforting her. "I be sorry for yer loss. I wish I'd been here sooner. Maybe I could have saved him."

Effie smiled and took his head in hers. It was just like Conall to believe he could fix everything in her life, to save her from the evils of their world. But the fact remained, some things in life were unfair no matter how hard you tried to fight it.

She kissed him, savoring his taste and the feel of his skin against hers. Every moment they spent together mattered, for she knew her life's purpose was about to change.

11

If there was one thing Conall Hamilton was sure of, he was madly in love with the woman in his arms. Her touch left his body wanting more, needing more. And her skin was like wine, smooth on the lips and felt like silk going down, leaving behind an erotic taste.

Looking into her eyes, the green tones reminded him of the Highland countryside touched by spring. If he looked closely enough he could see a secluded home with gray smoke billowing off into the sky, a few sheep dotting the green, grassy land, and mayhap a wee bairn or two running amuck. Aye, when he looked into Effie's eyes, he saw home.

Even though the physical attraction was strong between them, he loved her feisty spirit. Hell, if he was completely honest, his love had grown stronger for her every day over the past five years. He'd just needed to let go of the past to see it.

"What are ye thinking?" Effie asked.

Conall reached into her hair, carefully pulling out the pins one by one. Long red spirals fell to her shoulders and cascaded down her back. He longed to feel the softness of those curls wrapped around his hands. "I be thinking about making love to me wife."

Effie peered down into the water. "Conall, I need to tell ye---"

"It can wait." Conall lifted her chin with his finger and whispered. "We dinnae have much time." He kissed her softly on the lips.

Conall could sense something was bothering her but soon he would make her forget about her worries. They would cross that bridge soon enough but not tonight.

Slowly, he began to remove the green ribbon from around her neck. Effie tried to stop him, but it was too late.

Conall jerked in surprise when he saw the handprint around her neck. "Who did this to ye? And tell me the truth," he demanded.

"Me tongue got the best of me and Tavish got upset. I should know better than to provoke him."

"It shouldn't matter what ye say, lass. No man should ever raise his hand to a woman. He will pay for this." Conall gently smoothed his hand over the bruises.

"Please Conall, dinnae let this ruin our night," Effie begged as she sat in front of him sliding her hands down the peaks and valleys of his chest then lower, until she reached his manhood. Ever so lightly she ran her hands down his full length and back up to the top.

Conall growled and leaned back, allowing her to pleasure his body with long, tantalizing strokes. Her touch was like magic to his skin. *God's blood, she felt like heaven.*

His dragon awoke, ready to claim her. The beast grew stronger and more determined to shift. The magic inside the dungeon had been strong, yet here they appeared to be beyond the magic's reach.

Effie leaned forward, kissing his neck as she quickened her strokes. The sensation of her wet shift pressed hard against his body left him feeling every delectable curve. As the heat of passion grew, Conall wrapped his arm around her waist, drawing her closer while his other hand grabbed her breast and squeezed, thumbing over her nipple. Effie sighed sweetly into his neck.

Conall could feel his release coming quick. He didn't want it to end but she felt too damn good to hold back. Her hands on his skin were like nothing he had ever felt before. She calmed his dragon but at the same time, brought out the beast in him.

All it took was one last stroke to send him over the edge. Conall plunged his hand through Effie's hair, threw his head back, and gave in to his release. Stars exploded behind his eyes and his body tingled all over.

After the last ripples of his orgasm had settled, he stood, taking Effie with him. He scooped her up. Shockwaves of pure raw desire racked his body. "I need to get ye out of that shift and into that bed."

Effie threw her arms around his neck. "Shouldn't we wrap yer wounds?"

Conall stepped out of the tub and placed her on her feet. "Make it fast. Ye have to the count of three and I'm already on two."

Quickly Effie ran over to the trunk at the foot of the bed and opened it. Tossing her dresses aside, she finally found a shift. As she walked back to Conall, she ripped the material into strips. She grabbed a nearby drying cloth and began to pat the area dry before she wrapped it. When she had barely finished, Conall whispered in her ear, "Three."

He growled and captured her lips. He grabbed the front of her shift and ripped it down the middle, letting it fall where it may.

Stepping back, he feasted his eyes on the most exquisite beauty he had ever seen. The soft glow of the fire cast a golden hue over her curvaceous body that glistened with water. His eyes followed a water droplet as it ran down her neck to the valley between her breasts and to her stomach. *Aye*, this woman was made for him.

Effie grinned, and that was his undoing. He picked her up and carried her to the four-poster bed that had been tempting him from the moment he entered the chamber.

Conall urged Effie back on the mattress and positioned himself between her legs. He kissed her cheeks and worked his way down her neck. Effie's body was under his control. How could one man make her body hum and crave his wicked touch?

Effie moaned as Conall caressed and suckled on her breasts, her arousal building. As he licked and caressed her stomach, Effie's body tensed, knowing where he was headed. Her hands plunged into his hair, holding on for dear life. Before he reached her patch of red curls, he kissed her bellybutton and looked up at her. "Effie, ye're a bonny lass and I love every inch of ye. I could kiss ye all day long."

Teasing and exploring her body until she begged for release was something Conall had mastered. It was as if she was his dragon's toy. He draped one of her legs over his shoulder and flashed her a mischievous grin.

"Is this where ye want me?" He ran his finger gently between the folds of her womanhood, keeping his eyes locked on her. Then he bent down and flicked his tongue over her pearl.

Effie moaned and shook her head. "Aye. Please, Conall, dinnae tease me."

"Och, lass I assure ye, I be no tease." He used his fingers and tongue in ways that would make the devil blush. Aye—he'd mastered her body.

"Dear God, Conall," she panted. She grabbed the furs on the bed, gripping them tightly. Her body tingled all over as she succumbed to her release.

Still recovering from the pleasure, Conall slid up her body and kissed her neck. "Now where do ye want me?"

Effie wrapped her legs around his waist and grabbed his arse. "I want ye to stop talking and make love to me."

With one hard thrust Conall buried himself to the hilt. He moved slowly at first, making sure she felt every tantalizing inch of him. Fervently, he kissed her as he repeated his delicious assault by increasing his rhythm. Effie tilted her hips up and pressed hard against Conall. "Oh. Conall. Dinnae stop."

He pumped harder and faster, and Effie met him thrust for thrust. Relentlessly, he demanded her body and soul to surrender to him. Passion rolled over them, powerful and raw. Their bodies tensed as they came together, and she knew in that moment that he belonged to her forever.

Neither one wanted to let go, but the chill in the air made Effie shiver. Conall rolled off of her and slipped the blankets and fur over them. Pulling her in close, he wrapped his strong arms around her. Effie had never felt more loved or cherished. She gave in to his embrace, laying her head on his chest.

"Ye know, lass..." He kissed the top of her head. "I could never tire of ye and I can no' live without ye."

Effie looked up at him. Her heart sank. She had to let him go. It was the only way to save him. Together they would never be free from Tavish's wrath.

She would marry Sir Henry and move to England and hope that one day Conall would understand. If he had never met her, he would never have been wrongfully accused of a crime. She blamed herself. But she would save him.

Effie kissed Conall sweetly on the lips. "Get some sleep, ye need to heal."

"Effie, promise me you'll stay away from Tavish."

"Aye."

"And let me handle our escape. I dinnae want ye in harm's way."

"Conall, I –"

He tightened his arms around her, letting her know the conversation wasn't up for negotiation. "Trust me. Dinnae get involved. It's too dangerous."

Effie nodded. There was no way in hell she was going to sit back and do nothing. She'd sacrifice her own happiness if it meant Conall's survival.

Before long, Conall slipped into his healing sleep. She stayed with him as long as she could.

Knowing she'd already been gone too long, consequences be damned, she had to get back to her chamber.

She peeked under Conall's bandage to check the wound before she left. To her relief, it was almost healed and so were the others. *Good, ready to shift and fight for his life.*

Effie quietly started to dress. Before she left, she laid his clothing next to the hearth to dry. Scooping up her basket, she made her way to the door. She turned back to look at her dragon one last time.

Tears welled up, but in her heart, she knew what she had to do. "Please forgive me," she whispered.

Effie quit the hideaway chamber and made her way back to the dungeon. She bumped into Neil as she closed the door behind her. Neil's scowl told her all she needed to know. "I know this was no' part of the deal, Neil. But he was hurt. I had to mend his wounds."

Neil crossed his arms over his chest. "Lass, ye're lucky the guards are still passed out. Now get to yer chamber."

Effie presented a key and said, "I've marked the path. Make sure he makes it back to his cell."

"I'll see to the prisoner."

"Neil, can I ask ye a question?"

"Aye."

"How many of yer men are still loyal to me father?"

"I would say a few hundred."

"And these men trust ye?"

"They would fight to hell and back in the name of Maxwell." Neil's brows furrowed with suspicion. "What are ye planning, lass?

Effie leaned close to Neil. "Ready yer men. Justice is about to be served."

∼

Tavish turned to the hearth. The sweet sounds of muffled pleas soothed his dark soul like a salve to a wound. Grabbing an iron poker, he placed the tip over the fire until it glowed. Then he turned to his victim.

Maggie was bound to a chair and stripped from the waist up. Tears streamed down her face as she begged to be freed.

Inches away from her flawless skin, Tavish taunted her with the hot poker. "Maggie, sweet beautiful Maggie." He clucked his tongue at her. "All ye have to do is tell me where me sister be?"

Maggie shook her head, still claiming she didn't know where Effie was.

Tavish took the gag off Maggie. "Tell me. Where is me sister?"

"Please, laird, I dinnae know."

Tavish gritted his teeth, the wench was lying. She was covering for his sister and she'd pay dearly. Tavish placed the poker inches away from Maggie's right breast. Her eyes widened. He pressed the tip of the poker to her skin, then trailed it down her breast.

Maggie screamed and jerked against the restraints.

"Where is she?" he demanded. "Ye two have grown close." He tightened his grip around the poker. "Now tell, wench! Where's Effie?"

Maggie shook her head. "Please…I."

Tavish wasted no time and stuck her again. "Lie to me and ye'll be punished. Let this be a reminder." He watched her skin melt as he branded a W across her chest. Her screams were like music to his ears. "Now everyone will know ye're a whore."

Throwing the poker into the hearth with frustration, Tavish ran his hands through his hair and began to pace. *Damn it! Where is Effie?* Sir Henry had been worried about her and had checked her chamber only to find out she wasn't there.

"The stupid whore is going to ruin everything," he hissed. He'd made excuses all night for his sister's absence, convincing Henry that he would find her.

Tavish took a seat in a dark corner of the room. He had everything under control. Effie would not jeopardize his future, he'd make sure of that. Sooner or later Effie had to return and when she did…well, they would have a talk.

∽

Leaving Conall was the hardest thing Effie had ever done. Deep inside she wanted to tell him everything. But her dragon would never let her go, and she loved him for it. Too much to let him suffer. If she did what her brother wanted, not only would she get far away from Tavish, he'd leave Conall alone. The best outcome for everyone.

There was no question about making the ultimate sacrifice. Sir Henry would protect her.

Effie finally reached her bedchamber and prayed that she hadn't been missed. She opened the door. Terror filled her as she stared at the gruesome scene; Maggie's burned and lifeless body tied to a chair. "Maggie!"

Effie raced to the young lass, afraid it was too late. She picked her head up and to her relief, Maggie was breathing. "Thank heaven ye're alive." As she swept Maggie's hair back from her face, her heart stilled. Blistering trails marked her skin. "Maggie, dear God!" Bending down in front of her, Effie said, "Who did this to ye?"

Someone grabbed Effie from behind. With one arm around her waist holding her still, Tavish twisted her hair around his hand and yanked her head back. "Where have ye been, whore?"

Once again, she had nearly cost someone their life.

"Sir Henry has been looking for ye. Said ye told him ye weren't feeling well, but when he came to check on ye, ye weren't here."

"I was in the chapel. Praying for da." She knew her lie would hold true. Tavish wouldn't dare step foot in God's house, for the fear he would go up in flames.

Aggravated, Tavish shoved Effie toward Maggie and she landed hard on her knees. He stalked the room as fury consumed him. "Ye will not ruin this for me. Ye do see what happens when ye provoke me." He pointed to Maggie's branded body.

Effie crawled to Maggie. She'd give anything to save the lass, to take on her pain and scars.

Tavish stalked over to Effie and leaned over her. "I know ye went to see the dragon," he seethed. "I hope ye said farewell because he's a dead man. Ye should have stayed away and not meddled in me affairs."

Meddled? "Ye've accused an innocent man of murder. Ye killed our father. How did ye become so evil, so cruel?"

Tavish glared down at her. "Life hardens ye, sister. Dinnae take it personally."

"What are ye going to do, Tavish? Ye can no' kill me, nor brand me. What would Sir Henry think of ye?"

Effie could see the hatred in his eyes, but she was right.

"I suggest ye leave before I inform Henry of the evil ye've inflicted on Maggie. He warned ye to never lay a hand on a woman."

Tavish raised his hand to slap her, but this time Effie didn't flinch. She stood her ground, daring him to strike. His hand stopped midair as if he had thought again about his reaction. Tavish pointed at her and scowled. "This is no' over, sister. I'm still yer chief." With that, he turned and left the bedchamber.

With haste she untied Maggie, apologizing profusely. "Oh Maggie, I be so sorry."

As difficult as it was, Effie managed to get Maggie over to the bed. Every time she touched the lass's body, she cried out in pain. How she wished Abigale was there. She'd know what to do. "Maggie." Effie brushed back her sweaty hair from her face. "I'll be right back. I'm going to fetch the healer."

Effie shut the door and rushed down the corridor. "God, please help Maggie," she begged. Maggie would be scarred for life because of her. She was innocent. Effie vowed Tavish would pay.

12

*J*ames the Black Douglas and Rory dismounted from their horses outside an alehouse in a village a few miles from Caerlaverock Castle. If he was going to find out what happened to his friends, this was the place to get answers. Mead had a way of making people talk.

James and Rory entered the tavern, then quickly separated. Rory mingled at the bar while James took to the shadows, keeping an eye on their surroundings.

James sat down at a vacant table in the corner and removed his hood. Before long, a serving wench set a tankard down in front of him and filled it with mead.

"Can I be of further use to ye?" The lass leaned in as she placed the tankard in front of James.

James caught a glimpse of her generous breasts. She was pretty and young; mayhap ten-and-eight, the same age Abigale was when they first met. "Nay, I'm a married man." James took the tankard and drank it down.

The wench leaned closer. "Och, look around. No one here seems to mind." She grinned.

Intrigued by her boldness, James reached in his satchel and

pulled out a bag of coin and tossed it on the table. The blonde smiled as if she had done her job well and landed a man for the night.

She reached for the bag but was stopped as James covered it with his hand. "Tell me something, lass. Why are ye here selling yer soul to strangers?"

Her smile faded. "I have no place to call me own. Mr. Dougal and his wife allow me to stay here and work for them but 'tis not enough for me daughter." Disgraced, she looked down at her apron.

"Ye have a daughter?"

"Aye."

"And what would yer daughter think of her mother selling herself for coin?"

The lass stood silent.

"And ye have no husband?"

The lass looked up at James. "No husband."

"Ye're a bonny lass and good for sacrificing yerself for yer daughter, but ye can do better than this, aye?"

"Aye." She sniffed back a tear.

"There's enough coin in this bag for ye and yer daughter to start over. But ye have to promise me ye'll never step foot in this place, nor any place like this again."

"Aye, sir, ye have me word."

"Good." James offered her the bag.

"Thank ye." She picked it up and hurried off.

James leaned back and took a long drink. It amused him how his life had changed in such a short time. A hardened man taking out his fury on the battlefield and running away from his past; he'd chased away all the people who cared for him. He'd thought it the only way to keep his loved ones safe. Hell, he even pushed his brother, Archie, away.

But everything changed when he met the auburn-haired lass at the loch. Inwardly James smiled. Abigale had showed him forgiveness and how it felt to be thoroughly loved. Now with a babe on the way, he would bet his prized hunting dogs that he would experience a whole new level of love.

He needed to be done with this journey and back home. He'd kill Conall if he made him miss the birth of his first born.

The door to the alehouse blew open, sending a bone-chilling breeze throughout the room. He regretted sending Conall to Caerlaverock. Yet who would have thought Conall would be under attack once he arrived. Sir Herbert Maxwell was loyal to King Robert and an ally to the Douglas. It made no sense. Hopefully Rory would return soon with some news that could help him piece together the facts.

It burned his arse that someone had betrayed him. It was bad enough Marcus had betrayed the clan and Dragonkine, forcing James to remove his dragon and exile him from Scotland. And now Scotland could very well be in danger if the ancient king returned.

Pulling his cloak tighter, he had a decision to make. Whatever he chose, it would affect him and Dragonkine. Their futures were at stake.

His best friend was arse-deep in trouble at Caerlaverock castle, he could sense it.

James had always been able to feel Conall, especially when he was distressed or in need. James's skin itched to shift and his dragon stirred relentlessly, wanting to wreak havoc on Clan Maxwell. With Abigale ready to go into labor, the idea of shifting and just setting Caerlaverock ablaze seemed the quickest and easiest solution. But that would cause deeper problems.

Rory returned with a dram of whiskey.

"Did ye find anything out?" James asked.

"Aye." Rory turned the chair around and straddled it.

James motioned for more mead. By the look on Rory's face, it was going to be a long night. "Out with it."

Rory scrubbed his chin and nodded to a lass at a nearby table. "According to Ina..." Rory winked and smiled at her. "Clan Douglas attacked the north tower of Caerlaverock a fortnight ago."

Bewildered, James's brows pinched together. "I gave no such orders."

A bar wench refilled their cups with mead.

"Excuse me, mistress," Rory called as she was leaving. "Would ye happen to have any provisions available? Mayhap some bread?"

"Aye. There be some stew left over from the evening meal. Would ye like for me to bring ye a bowl?"

"Aye, two." He looked at James who was growing more aggravated by the minute. "Would ye like a bowl?"

James waved her off and glared at Rory. "Our brother-in-arms is in danger and all ye can think about is yer stomach?"

"I can no' think clearly when me belly is growling."

James rolled his eyes. "Rory, is that all the information ye received?"

"Nay, during the attack, Sir Herbert was murdered by the commander. He's been captured and awaits punishment."

"Conall," James whispered.

"Aye, but there's more," Rory said. "There's to be trial by combat."

"At Caerlaverock?"

"Aye, in the courtyard." Rory grabbed his tankard and drank.

For a moment they fell silent as the wench returned with two bowls of stew.

Rory flashed her his irresistible smile, making the lass go weak in the knees.

Wasting no time, Rory spooned the stew into his mouth. "So, what are we going to do?"

James leaned forward with his elbows resting on the table. "If we have already been accused of this attack, then I say we attack and get Conall the hell out of there."

"And what is our strategy?"

James's features darkened. "We shift."

Rory dropped his spoon into his bowl and stew splattered over the table. His surprised expression slipped into an approving grin.

Both men picked up their mead, wrapped their revealed talons around the tankards, ready for battle.

13

How in the bloody hell was he going to get off this mountain? Marcus stood by the ice cave entrance observing the land below. Deep in the valley on the north side of the mountain, the land was covered in snow. Fog rolled in slowly, casting a sense of gloom everywhere. Pulling the fur tight around his body, the Highlander stared into a cloud of nothingness, mourning his dragon.

Having once been an ice dragon, he took comfort in the cave and swore he could feel the snow healing him. Perhaps he was even gaining strength. Marcus exhaled, his breath a string of smoke in the frigid air. How did he manage to make it this high up on the mountain? His horse wouldn't have been able to tolerate the steep incline. Hell, he was even surprised he wasn't freezing, being a vulnerable human.

The rumbling of his stomach echoed through the empty cave, reminding him he needed food. With no strength to hunt, he staggered to a pool of water where an icicle dripped from the ceiling. He bent down, cupped his hands, and took a long drink. He could feel the energy draining from his body. Weakened with despair and hunger, he crawled to the rear of the cave where he'd been sleeping.

Marcus drifted in and out of sleep, losing touch with reality as fever coursed through his body. At one point, he swore Abigale was there taking care of him. But as he reached for her, she vanished.

He opened his eyes as he heard a sound coming from the entrance of the cave. At first, it looked to be a raven, but as the image came closer he quickly changed his mind. The winged creature was a dragon.

The beast landed and its wings disappeared. It transformed into a human wearing black armor. Marcus sat up as he watched three more dragons fly in right behind the black knight.

"Creeping death," Marcus whispered in disbelief.

"I see yer healing," the knight said through his helm as he assessed Marcus's condition.

Marcus slowly stood, fearing for his life. "Are ye the reason I'm here?"

The armored knight nodded.

"Why am I not dead?"

"Marcus, you cannot die. Our king needs you. Needs us to fulfill his wishes. We brought you here to heal."

Marcus didn't quite understand. If he was to fulfill the king's wishes, then why didn't the creepers help him kill James when they had the chance? "I do no' understand. If we are to awaken our king, why didnae yer men help me kill James? We had him in our grasp."

The knight was hard to read with his helm shut, his eyes were the only thing that showed. "I need to explain. You are the only one who can awaken the king. We cannot interfere, shed blood on holy ground. That is your destiny alone, Marcus."

Marcus drew deeper into his fur as he continued to listen.

"We are here to make sure you succeed. We can heal you, help plan the course of action, but we cannot kill a dragon under any circumstances. If a human gets in the way...." The knight paused.

Marcus heard the violence in his tone. Now that Marcus was human, he should tread softly around these beasts.

"But I do no' have a dragon anymore. How can I fulfill me destiny when me dragon has been taken away?"

The three death dragons that had been silently standing by parted and a woman came into view. She was cloaked in fur from head to toe. As he met her gaze, he noticed she'd been crying and feared for her life. She wasn't there of her own free will.

The knight walked over to the woman and shoved her toward Marcus and she stumbled to the ground. "I've brought you a gift."

The last thing on Marcus's mind was sex. He didn't need or want a woman when food and ale would do him better. He was too weak to perform.

Beyond his body being broken, his soul was crushed. A human betrayed him, killing his sister. His dragon was dead. Aye, bedding a woman was the last thing he wanted to do. "I dinnae need a woman."

The knight yanked the woman to her feet. A whimper escaped her lips. He ripped the fur cloak from her body, leaving her naked and exposed.

Like any man, he couldn't resist looking at her. There was no denying her beauty. Her hair was long and the color of honey. Brown eyes met his and something moved him inside. This was no ordinary lass.

As he walked closer and moved her hair aside, revealing her breasts, she tensed. As if in some kind of trance, he reached out and touched her arm. She trembled at his touch as Celtic designs appeared on her skin the more he touched her. Tears streamed down her cheeks.

"She's one of our females," Marcus said in disbelief.

"Aye, she's yer female Kine. She's here to help ye heal," the knight said as he shoved the woman into Marcus's arms.

He caught her and wrapped his fur around her.

"She will help restore your dragon."

As soon as their naked bodies connected it was like magic pulsing over his skin. The blood pumping through his veins might be cold, but he was on fire. The more his body touched hers, the more his ability to hold back crumbled. Marcus aggressively pulled her closer and nuzzled his face into her neck as she tried to wiggle free.

Something took over and he couldn't release her. His dragon was feeding off her magic, healing him.

He laid down on his furs, taking the female with him. She fought him as he pulled her close. Drunk with magic, he drained her until she weakened. Soon, his dragon would be fully healed. He smiled as he whispered against her skin, "I will no' forget yer service. Thank ye, lass."

14

After Conall's night with Effie, his body healed and his dragon felt stronger. As he sat up, he realized he was back in the dungeon. He knew by the smell.

Rubbing his hands down his face, he wondered how long he had been asleep, although his body and senses told him that it hadn't been long. That sweet honey scent still lingered on his skin and the taste of her burned him to the core. His cock hardened as he remembered her hands wrapped round his length and those sweet torturous kisses still pricked his skin. His dragon purred from her soothing touch. Leaning his head back, he closed his eyes and called forth an image of his red-headed lass. Christ, she was beautiful.

But there was something missing. As a mated Dragonkine, Conall could feel Effie and sense her feelings, though he couldn't read her mind. She was filled with sorrow and worried about something. Knowing she mourned for her father, he had expected to feel grief, yet this was different. She was keeping something from him. It felt wrong. She felt distant. It was just like Effie to hide, keeping her burdens to herself.

If only his dragon was at full strength, last night they could've escaped this hell, but he didn't want to risk it. He had to protect Effie. He needed more time to fully heal.

The magic binding his cell stifled his dragon once again. It struggled to surface, to express itself. Which made Conall restless. Needing to stretch his legs, he stood but couldn't walk far. An ankle chain kept him close to the wall. He grabbed the chain and pulled with all his might. The damn thing wouldn't budge. God's wounds, he wished he had full power.

The dungeon door opened, and heavy footsteps sounded in the corridor outside his cell. He looked around for Caden, but he was nowhere in sight. The shadowy corners were perfect places to hide.

Tavish and four guards arrived. A guard opened the cell door and two more guards rushed in and pinned Conall to the wall. How Conall wanted to destroy them—rip them apart piece by piece.

Caden stepped out of the shadows and the other guards threw him to the ground with swords drawn. "Cowards," Caden shouted as one of them kicked him in the ribs.

Conall didn't struggle. The magic suppressing his dragon and strength made him easy to control. He'd save his energy for the right moment.

But when Effie's vile brother stepped into the cell, hatred overwhelmed Conall. The bastard had dared to touch his woman, and he would pay—suffer greatly for it. There was a special place in hell for a man like Tavish. And Conall would make damn sure he would walk through those fiery gates.

"I see me sister has been to see ye." Tavish strolled over.

With a blade pressed to his neck, Conall couldn't challenge him.

"Did the whore tell ye about her good news?"

Conall glared at him.

"Of course, she did," Tavish mocked.

"Nay," Conall lied. He didn't know what kind of games he was playing, and refused to play along.

"Och, I'm baffled. I would think she would want ye to know she's to wed Sir Henry." Tavish nodded to one of the guards, and he punched Conall in the ribs. Conall took the blow silently and willingly, giving Tavish no satisfaction.

Inside, Conall and his dragon fumed with rage. Was this the reason why he had felt distance between himself and Effie? His soul shook as he thought about his red-haired lass with another man.

Tavish nodded again, and another blow pummeled his ribs, giving him matching aches on both sides of his body. His knees threatened to buckle. "Me people want justice. A trial by combat is in order. Ye will pay for killing me father."

Conall glared at Tavish. "Ye're mad. A delusional bastard. I didnae kill yer father." Conall sucked in a breath, fighting back the black magic. "Ye will pay for this treachery."

Tavish's eyes darkened. "Ye have no choice. Either Henry will behead ye or ye submit and return to the dungeon where eventually yer dragon will die." Tavish unsheathed his dirk. "Ye see, ye'll be too weak to fight and by the time the wedding is over, the magic will have killed yer dragon. It's that simple. Ye will die one way or another." In one fluid motion, Tavish drove the dirk hard into Conall's stomach and twisted the blade.

Conall cried out as gut-wrenching pain ripped through him. His head flopped forward.

Tavish grabbed a fist full of Conall's hair and shoved his head back. "Just ask yer friend over there. He can tell ye how it feels." Tavish ripped his dirk out of Conall's body and let go of his head. He motioned for the guards to follow him out of the cell.

As the magic took over his body, Conall dropped to the ground holding his stomach.

"That bastard needs to be put in his place," Caden seethed.

Conall looked up to see his cellmate's reptilian eyes. "Ye're Dragonkine?"

"Fight the magic." Caden helped Conall off the floor. "Ye have a Sassenach to kill."

15

*E*ffie stood in front of the mirror and combed through her hair in a daze. The sheer nightdress she wore hung loosely off her shoulders and left nothing to imagination. From the outside, she appeared as happy as a newly wedded woman should, but inside she was numb.

A kiss on the back of her neck brought her attention to the man standing behind her. His strong arm snaked around her waist, pulling her against his body in a loving embrace. Moving her hair to one side, he exposed more of her slender neck and continued to trail kisses just below her ear. "You're exquisite," Sir Henry whispered. "I knew you'd make me a beautiful wife."

Effie faked a smile and carried on brushing her hair.

Henry took the comb from her hand and stepped in front of her. "I feel as though ye've been avoiding me."

Aye, she had. She'd already asked him about his family in which he took great pleasure in telling her about his wealth. It had bought her some time, but not enough. She was quickly running out of excuses to delay the consummation of their marriage.

Sir Henry unlaced the front of her nightdress. Effie grabbed his hands. "I would like to bathe first."

Henry exhaled in frustration. "I'm not the first man ye've bedded."

Effie paused.

"Ye're brother told me about your past." Henry leaned in and whispered in her ear. "I know ye're a whore."

Effie's heart raced as he grabbed her arms. She swallowed hard, keeping her composure.

"No more games. Ye will bed me now."

Effie let go of his hands and glared at him. She debated telling him exactly how she felt. She'd never love him, not the way she loved Conall. Henry could have her body, but her heart was already taken.

"Do as ye wish." Effie stood in front of him, hate glaring in her eyes. If this was what she had to endure for Conall's safety, she'd make the sacrifice. With her in England, far away from her dragon, Tavish couldn't touch either one of them. *If* her plan worked.

Henry cupped her breasts, squeezing a little too hard. She closed her eyes and imagined it was Conall touching her, kissing her neck. As she gave herself to Henry, she repeated her prayer she'd said before the wedding, "*Dear God,*" she prayed to herself, "*please forgive me for what I'm about to do, for I do it out of love. I know it's too late for me, but please keep Conall safe.*"

Henry lifted her nightdress. She clutched her stomach, feeling overwhelmingly sick as she pushed him away. Bile quickly rose up her throat.

Concerned, Henry asked, "What's wrong?"

"I'm going to be sick." Effie held her hand over her mouth.

Henry quickly retrieved the water basin from the nightstand. He dumped the water just in time for her to vomit. Her stomach swirled like a raging storm and she vomited again.

Effie peered up from the bowl to find Henry's head turned to the side with his eyes clamped shut. His skin was pale, and he made a heaving sound as if he too was going to get sick, too. A brave knight that couldn't handle the sight of his bride retching. It humored her.

Effie took the bowl from Henry and placed it outside the chamber door. Grabbing a cloth, she dampened it with water from the pitcher and washed her face. As she turned to Henry, he stood like a stone statue, still pale.

"Henry, I'm sorry. It must be something I ate."

"Aye." Sweat beaded his forehead. "Should I go and fetch the healer?"

"Nay, I just need to rest."

Henry made his way out of the chamber.

As she slipped into bed, she found comfort that tonight she'd escaped consummating their marriage.

~

A voice hummed in Conall's head as he tried to wake, but his body refused to respond to the command. The pain from the gash in his gut pulsed. He called for his dragon but was left unanswered. The magic was too powerful inside the cell walls, it weakened him and his dragon.

"Conall, wake up!" Caden called out, shaking his shoulder. The urgency in his voice rang clear. "Ye need to get up. Now!"

Cold water in his face shocked him awake finally.

Caden threw the cup across the cell. "Ye dinnae have much time, the guards are coming for ye. There's been chatter all morn about the battle and how ye have to fight today." The blond warrior squatted in front of Conall.

"This is no' good." He shook his head as he examined the fresh wound on his stomach. "'Tis no' healing. I've done all I can do." Frustrated, he ran his hand through his hair. After the beating Tavish had inflicted, Caden had spent most of the night tending Conall's wound. He was in no shape to fight.

Conall slapped his hand away. "I can take care of meself." With a grunt, Conall painstakingly rose to his feet, stumbling about the small space. The chains had been removed from his feet, although he felt like they still drug behind him, heavy and unforgiving. He braced his hand on the stone wall for balance as he shook the cobwebs from his mind. The last thing he remembered was the dirk puncturing his skin and the thought of Effie with Sir Henry, married.

Rage tore through him, whirling like a gust of wind. His dragon stirred, rattling his cage, desperate to shift. He hungered for blood and would soon quench his appetite. No one came between a Dragonkine and his mate and lived to tell the tale.

Two guards fumbled with the keys to his cell as they bantered about how Tavish had outwitted a dragon. Conall turned his head and flashed his reptilian eyes, causing both to step back in fear.

"Step out where I can see ye and place yer hands in front," one guard demanded.

Confident, Conall stepped out of the cell, giving them plenty of room to enter his lair if they so dared. With his stance firm, he held his hands together in front.

The second guard opened the cell door and the other guard scurried in. With shaking hands, he slapped the metal cuffs, attached to a thick, heavy chain, around Conall's wrists. The warrior stared down at the man, amused by his distress.

Conall stayed calm, for he desperately needed to escape the magic bound to the cell, so he could heal.

He cleared his throat. "Where are ye taking me?"

"It be time for battle."

"Battle? Do I have a squire to assist me?"

"Squire?" The guard questioned as if it was an odd request.

"In a trial by combat the accused and champion receive the right of a squire. I will have weapons, as I'm sure Sir Henry will, too. I need a squire to bring me weapons."

The guard snickered. "If ye want a squire, look around." He pointed to the folks in their cells. Half the men were either too sick or weak to pick up a weapon. "If ye trust a thief, go ahead, choose yer squire."

"Caden, do ye accept to be me squire?" He didn't know if he could trust his cellmate but he had to take the chance, for if Caden was what he suspected, this fight would be over as soon as it started. Being as weak as he was, Conall didn't have the strength to beat Henry, but with Caden there, he had a better chance. He knew he was taking a risk. Caden could try to escape and leave him behind.

Stepping out of the shadows, Caden cracked his fingers and rolled his neck. "Aye."

The guard holding the door commanded the other guard to chain Caden.

The blond warrior stood shoulder-to-shoulder with Conall and placed his hands in front of him.

Keeping his eyes locked in front of him, Conall said, "Dinnae make me regret me decision."

As Caden smirked, Conall knew he had made the right decision.

One guard led from the front and the other pushed the prisoners ahead from behind as the entourage shuffled down the dark corridor. The pathway opened into the courtyard where Clan Maxwell was gathered, awaiting the battle. Conall was exhausted and could barely stand by the time they reached the locked gate separating them from the crowd. One of the guards pushed Conall forward, and he stumbled into Caden, then fell to the floor.

"Ye must stay strong," Caden said as he helped Conall up. "Yer red-headed lass needs ye."

Conall balanced against the stone wall. The will of his dragon was much stronger than his human side. He reached down deep, pushing away any thoughts of defeat. Effie needed him.

"Ye maggots wait here until the gate opens. Then the fun begins." The guard chuckled as he slammed the cage door shut.

Caden and Conall gazed at the courtyard through the gaps in the bars. There had to be at least five hundred people, if not more. Conall leaned his back against the bars, supporting his weight and catching his breath. He must fight the black magic immobilizing his dragon. He must stay strong.

A man dressed in a hooded cloak approached and unlocked the gate and their restraints. "Yer weapons are on the table. The squire stays with me until yer weapon needs replacing." The hooded man stepped closer to Conall. The foulness of his breath turned his stomach. "Test me and ye shall meet me sword."

Conall fisted his hands, tamping down the urge to shove the bastard. This fight wasn't with him. He reminded himself to save his strength for Henry.

Conall walked over to the table. He picked up a wooden targe that looked like it had seen many battles. He'd be lucky if the hunk of wood would last the first round. Passing over the battle axes, he picked up a claymore. He tested his grip. Even though he knew Sir Henry's weapon selection would be to his advantage, Conall had the confidence of a Highlander. The appearance of a sword didn't guarantee a win, it was how you used it.

As he looked up to the second level of the curtain wall, people were pushing their way to find the best view. Further away, he noticed a canopied balcony with clan Maxwell's flag whipping in the wind along with a red-crossed flag indicating clan Maxwell had indeed sided with the English.

His heart sank when Effie came into view. She was beautiful in a deep-green dress and with her fiery hair blowing in the wind. How he wanted her—to go to her and... An armored knight with his helmet tucked under his arm bent down and kissed her.

As he watched Henry deepen the kiss, Conall's rage took over and his dragon summoned a storm. The wind picked up. Gray clouds rolled in like charging warhorses in the sky. Thunder boomed and rattled the earth as rain suddenly fell. Aye, his dragon was back.

"Are you feeling better this morn, my lady?" Henry lifted Effie's chin and examined her face.

"Aye." She faked a smile, knowing full well she would have to give herself to her husband soon. Fortunately, he had stayed away after she had gotten sick. But the look in his eyes told her he was ready to bed her. If she didn't love Conall... Sir Henry was a handsome and charming man and would likely make a good husband. But no one could replace Conall. And Effie refused to betray her dragon.

"Good. I still think you should see the healer after the battle." It was more a demand then a request.

"I will," she said, pretending to be a proper wife.

That made him smile and he kissed her cheek, then made his way to the courtyard.

She took her seat under the canopy and looked nervously down where the fight would take place. She prayed her plan to free Conall would work. If he was healed and able to shift, all would be well. The difficult part would be convincing him to leave without her.

She took a deep breath as she eyed Sir Neil. He nodded, which gave her the reassurance that everything was in place. The Maxwell loyalists, the ones who served her father fearlessly, were beside him. She closed her eyes, relieved. Soon Conall would be free.

"It won't be long now before yer dragon dies," Tavish whispered. Startled, Effie's eyes opened wide. He sat down next to her, causing bile to rise in her throat.

"Och, I do think ye be mistaken, Tavish, me dragon *will* be leaving here today."

He bellowed with laughter. "Ye have no idea who ye're dealing with, do ye sister?"

Of course, she did. She was dealing with a good-for-nothing pain in her arse bastard who she wished had never come into her life. In fact, she regretted not standing up for herself all those years ago, and all the missed opportunities to enlighten her father as to what a monster his son had become.

As she turned to face Tavish, she realized this was the man who could ruin everything her father had worked so hard for. He would turn all the good Maxwell warriors away, give in to the temptation of greed, and destroy their good family name.

But she had seen an even darker side of Tavish that chilled her to the marrow. What he had done to Maggie was unforgiveable. She was innocent, and Tavish had taken that away. Plus, knowing he very well could have killed her father, left her more fearful for her life. She knew pushing her brother too far might make him snap.

Tavish stood and raised his hands. The crowd settled down. The power he held over her clan made her sick. The Maxwell's deserved better than this.

"Good morn to ye fine folk of Dumfries. Justice will be served here, as me father's murderer will be punished and put to death."

The crowd roared like savage animals.

It was a disgrace, Effie thought. These people were so quick to pass judgment upon an innocent man when the true murderer stood before them. Even though she couldn't prove it, she knew Tavish had done it. These people weren't looking for justice.

Effie ignored the crowd as her brother carried on. She had a plan and needed to make sure everything was ready. Over on the east battlements she saw Neil in place, and although she couldn't identify his men, she knew they walked among the crowd at different vantage points with their weapons ready for battle.

After she was satisfied that everything was falling into place, she closed her eyes and tried to speak with Conall through mind-speak. If he was nearby, she should be able to communicate with him.

"Conall, can ye hear me?"

Silence.

"Let the battle begin!" Tavish's voice rang over the crowd and Effie shuddered. If this plan didn't work, everyone she loved could very well end up dead.

16

The crowd roared as Sir Henry took his place on the field. With his sword drawn and shield raised, he looked like a true knight ready to fight.

The black-cloaked man shoved Conall out of the archway and into the courtyard. As weak as he was, he fell to his hands and knees.

The crowd booed and cursed while they threw rotten vegetables at him.

Sir Henry lowered his weapon and turned around, addressing the crowd. "Is this the man I'm to battle? This weak coward-of-a-man? I'd thought a Scot better than that." He pointed to Conall, mocking him as the crowd applauded.

Just as a cabbage narrowly missed Conall's head, he grabbed his dull weapon and slowly rose to his feet, squaring his shoulders and spitting the dirt from his mouth. "And I dinnae expect much from an Englishman."

With all his strength, he met Henry in the middle of the courtyard.

Henry broke the silence first. "Do you intend to fight me with a blade like that?"

Conall stared at the weapon. "I dinnae need a blade." He threw it to the ground.

Henry chuckled. "You Scots are more stupid than I realized. With a little work and training, Effie will make me a fine English lady. I must assure you, I'll take good care of the lass when you're gone."

Anyone could make empty threats; 'twas actions that mattered. Conall drew closer to Henry. "Did ye know she's already married? She's married to me." He pushed off of Henry, sending him stumbling back.

Visibly enraged, Henry charged Conall with his sword, lunging the blade toward his chest. Conall dodged out of the way, sending Henry running past him. But before Conall could face his opponent, Henry sliced the back of his leg, causing him to go down on one knee.

With a cocky swagger, Henry walked behind Conall and grabbed a fistful of his hair. He yanked Conall's head back and placed his blade on his throat. "Told you I'd kill you this day."

Conall sank his elbow into Henry's gut. He repeated the move until Henry was forced to let go of his hair.

Out of the corner of his eye, Conall saw the hooded man's head roll into the courtyard. He looked up and Caden was there holding the man's swords. He stepped over the headless body and slid Conall the weapon.

Caden gave him a nod, and Conall knew he had already won the day.

Conall grabbed the sword and squared off with Henry again. Equally armed now, their weapons met in midair and they struggled for dominance. Taking advantage of Conall's lack of armor, Henry took a cheap shot, kneeing him between the legs.

Conall doubled over in obvious pain, and Henry hit him again, bashing Conall in the face sending him to the ground. Once again, the Englishman seized the moment and swiftly drew his sword, pressing it against Conall's throat. Conall swallowed against the cold steel and scanned the crowd. That's where he found her, his lovely Effie terrified and on her feet, screaming his name.

Effie couldn't believe her eyes when she saw how badly wounded Conall looked. What had happened? Surely, he had healed! By the love of saints, she prayed he could still shift. He had to shift if he was going to make it out of there alive.

Tavish leaned over and squeezed her arm. "I told ye, whore, ye have no idea who ye're dealing with."

Effie sat on the edge of her seat as Conall and Henry clashed again. Conall was too weak to fight, and it sickened her the way her people were treating an innocent man. She closed her eyes and tried to reach Conall, but there was no response. The magic had to be blocking her. He had to shift. It was an integral part of her plan. Without him shifting, Neil was going to have a hard time holding back the English garrison. She had to help Conall, regardless of the risks.

As Henry hovered over Conall's body with a sword pointed at his neck, Effie stood and screamed for Conall to shift.

The crowd grew quiet. Suddenly, gray clouds rolled in and the wind picked up. If she listened close enough, Effie swore she heard the sound of flapping wings. Gazing at the sky, she could not see anything unusual. As she turned her attention back to the courtyard, shadows in the shape of dragon wings moved across the courtyard. Could it be? She prayed it was true—so desperately needed it to be…

Two dragons made a hard landing. Perched high on the west side of the curtain wall, the great beasts roared, shaking everything in sight.

Women and men alike screamed in fear, some running away, others cowering. 'Twas like the devil had come to claim their souls. Several people were trampled underfoot as chaos descended on the fleeing people.

Effie sucked in a breath, hope suddenly blooming in her heart. She had seen Conall in dragon form, but never the others. The black dragon with glowing red under-scales was massive and menacing. There was no doubt that dragon was James—Abigale's husband. The other dragon was vibrant green and when it roared, the earth shook, sending Sir Henry to the ground. The dragon must be Rory!

The dragons flew from the battlements, blowing fire and smoke, scattering Sir Henry's garrison. Effie looked toward the east battlement and nodded to Neil. It was time she got Conall out of there.

Effie was about to fight her way to the courtyard when Tavish grabbed her arm and pulled her behind him as he made his way through the hectic stream of panicked people. "Ye dinnae know when to stop, do ye!" He shoved her forward with a dagger pointed at her side.

Tavish was too strong for her to fight but she would not give up. She screamed out to Conall and tried to connect with him through mind speak. *Shift, Conall, please!*

～

Smoke surrounded Sir Henry in the courtyard. Though he had lost his sword when he hit the ground to escape the dragon fire, he'd managed to stay calm, focusing on Conall. Nothing would keep him from destroying him. He stalked over to him and landed a brutal blow, his fist connecting with Conall's jaw. The force blurred Conall's vision and he was disoriented. But he could have sworn he heard Effie's voice, even though she was far away. "Shift, Conall, please!" He blinked, trying to recover.

Then he felt a blast of power inside, it radiated up his body, lighting every muscle. His brothers were there. The dragon deep inside of him felt it, too, and paced relentlessly as he waited for the invisible bars keeping him imprisoned to crumble and set him free.

Conall managed to get to his knees while Henry eyed the flying dragons and issued orders to what men he had left in the area. That's when Conall noticed Henry's armor had started to disintegrate, turning a copper color with small holes appearing. What would cause such a thing to happen? 'Twasn't his dragon brothers in the sky...

Standing behind Henry was a white-scaled dragon with green eyes intensely focused on Sir Henry.

"Caden?" Conall said, feeling an instant connection with the beast.

"Who else would be daft enough to stick around?" the dragon answered through mind-speak.

Conall smiled. Never in his life had he been happier to see his Kine. Even though there were many questions that needed to be answered about Caden, they would have to wait.

Finally finding the strength, Conall stood and stared down at Henry who was left speechless and motionless from shock. "Ye English should never underestimate the Highland dragon." Reaching deep within his soul, remembering every violent act and all the suffering his brethren had suffered at the hands of the English and humans, including the loss of his beloved wife and son, Conall called forth his dragon. It was a fierce and humbling experience as his scales erupted, first up his spine, then down his arms and legs.

Conall threw his head back and screamed as razor-sharp talons replaced his fingers. Aye, he was a storm dragon through and through.

He swept his barbed tail underneath Sir Henry's feet. Before the knight knew what had happened, he was lying on the ground, paralyzed by fear.

Blazing arrows whizzed through the air, some landing in Conall's thick-scaled skin. But they couldn't penetrate his dragon armor. As he called to the skies, the clouds responded. Lightening flashed overhead, then the torrential rains...

Sir Henry crawled to cover, obviously defeated. Conall watched him signal his men to retreat. At least the bastard knew when to give up. Conall's fight wasn't really with the English knight, not yet anyway. He had a more important monster to kill...Tavish.

"Conall!"

He turned to where Effie had been sitting but she was gone, along with Tavish. He growled and searched the crowd. He would have to follow her voice. "Effie, lass, can ye hear me?"

"Aye, thank God ye can hear me," Effie said.
"Where are ye? I'm coming for ye."
"South tower. Tavish... He's going to kill me."

Conall looked toward the south tower and his heart sank. If he didn't reach that tower, his life would never be the same again. He roared in desperation and fear as he took to the sky.

17

Tavish pushed Effie up the narrow stairway of the south tower. "Ye couldn't leave things be, worthless whore!" She'd seen her brother mad before but not like this. Hatred radiated off him.

"I had this all worked out." He kicked her when she stopped to take a breath. "End father's life so I could become laird, then marry ye off to a powerful English lord to keep ye out of the way."

As they reached the top of the tower, Tavish shoved Effie toward the battlement wall. He paced in front of her, raking his hand through his hair. "I've done everything right, even tried to give ye a decent future. But ye destroyed it, ye thankless bitch."

"Tavish, ye've built yer house out of lies and murder."

Tavish hovered close to her. "Aye. I hated him."

Effie closed her eyes, trying hard not to cry. How her father must have suffered. "But why? Ye were his only son, next in line as chief. Surely ye had nothing to gain by killing him?"

"Me sweet sister, ye really dinnae know."

"What?" Confusion set in, along with a little panic—just what was her brother capable of, how deep did his evil go?

"I'm father's bastard. I can never be chief as long as ye're alive. I thought by marrying ye off to Sir Henry, I'd gain not only a powerful ally, but ye'd be far away from here, living in England. Ye'd no longer be a threat."

"Tavish, I-"

Tavish held his hand over her mouth to silence her. "Why couldn't ye have done what ye were told?"

Effie couldn't believe it. All these years her family had kept this secret from her. Tavish was a bastard. Now she understood his motives. He had tried to break her physically and emotionally so she could never be chieftain.

Tavish pressed her harder into the wall, the rough edges of the stone biting her back.

The wind blew and there was a chill in the air. A loud clap of thunder broke, shaking the structure. Effie desperately needed to find a way to escape. She turned her head to the side, looking down from the tower. If she jumped, she'd die.

People were running on the upper curtain wall. Sir Henry came into view as he mounted his warhorse and rode off. The Maxwell army was trying to control the people whilst defending themselves from the English soldiers. Caerlaverock Castle was in complete chaos.

As she looked to the center of the courtyard, a silver dragon landed and stared at her. She could hear Conall. She smiled, knowing that her dragon was free.

Pain ripped through her head as Tavish grabbed her by the hair. "Please Tavish," she pleaded, trying to squirm loose. "I have no desire to be clan chief. I am no threat to ye."

He forced her to the edge of the wall, her head hanging over the ledge. "Please, Tavish! Dinnae do this!"

Tavish squeezed her throat. "I dinnae believe ye. Ye turned me men against me and started a rebellion with Sir Neil. Tell me, Effie, did ye really think ye'd get away with it?"

"I...had to save Conall!"

His evil laugh chilled her. "Ye will pay for me losses here tonight."

He lifted Effie up by the neck until her feet no longer touched the ground, cutting off her ability to breathe steadily. Through the dizziness that descended on her, she fought to get ahold of the dagger she'd hidden up her sleeve.

With one fluid motion, she stabbed her brother underneath the ribcage. She twisted the blade and forced it deeper into his body, until she felt it strike bone.

Shocked and angered by her attack, Tavish pushed her off the ledge.

In one hopeless attempt, she clutched at the air and prayed for a miracle as the top of the tower grew smaller. She was going to die.

Even though her every instinct told her to panic and fight for her life, she let go.

Closing her eyes, the air felt light around her as if she was floating. She made peace with God and thanked Him for the time she'd had with Conall. Not everyone could say that they had been truly and fully loved by another. Not everyone found true love and for that she had been blessed, even though it had only been for five short years.

She was thankful for the courage she had shown, rebelling against her brother. It warmed her heart knowing she would see her mum and da again, for she knew Neil would make sure she rested alongside of the lord and lady of Caerlaverock Castle. Tavish on the other hand, would burn in hell for the evil he'd brought upon their family. And, for that reason alone, she could rest in peace.

"I got ye, lass."

She opened her eyes and met Conall's gaze—her dragon's gaze.

"'Tis a fine day for flying, aye?"

Relief flooded Effie's body as she held on for dear life, ever grateful she loved a dragon.

～

With a few pumps of his wings, Conall caught the wind and flew them back up to the battlements. He didn't want to think about how he almost hadn't made it to Effie in time. Time had stood still as he watched the love of his life falling from the tower. Never in his life had he felt as helpless as he did standing there watching. Thank the gods his dragon instincts kicked in.

As soon as he'd taken flight, Caden was right there with him. It seemed as though he owed this stranger for helping him, yet there were questions that needed answering, like how in the hell he ended up in the Maxwell dungeon, and why he had been keeping his dragon a secret. Right now, he wanted to focus on the lass in his arms.

"Are ye alright?"

She didn't answer, only stared at him with empty eyes. She was going into shock.

"Effie, love, stay with me. Ye're going to be all right. I've got ye."

Banking to the right, Conall flew in with a soft landing, careful not to jostle Effie. He set her on her feet and she stumbled. "Easy lass."

That's when he caught sight of Tavish lying on the ground face up in a pool of blood with a dagger in his hands. The bastard had gotten what he deserved, yet he wished he was the one carrying the burden of stabbing him, not Effie.

Transforming back into human form, he wrapped Effie up in his arms and held her as Caden made his landing a few feet behind them, still in dragon form.

"Lass, talk to me. I need to know ye are well."

With her back to her brother's body, she asked, "Is he dead?"

"Aye."

She looked up at Conall and the sadness in her eyes nearly shattered his heart. "I killed me brother?"

"Nay, ye defended yerself. Dinnae allow him to make ye feel guilty. He was going to kill ye. I saw him push ye off the edge of the battlements."

"And ye…" She took his face in her shaking hands. "Ye saved me." Tears streamed down her cheeks.

"Och, lass, we still have a wedding to plan. I surely can no' do that on me own." He smiled.

For a brief moment she smiled back; however, it was replaced by guilt. Stepping out of his embrace, she shook her head and said, "Conall, I'm already married to Sir Henry. I had to... Tavish--"

"I do no' blame ye, lass." Conall's jaw tightened. "I do believe ye said aye to me first. And I do recall," he leaned toward her until his lips brushed against her ear, "we sealed our vows by making love."

She nodded, her expression revealing hope.

"I would bet me dragon on it that Sir Henry will no longer show his face around here after seeing four dragons. He'll favor annulment."

"Aye," she agreed.

"Good thing, lass. Ye have nothing to worry about."

"Conall, before I stabbed Tavish, he told me that he was me father's bastard and that I was the rightful heir. That's why he killed me father and planned to marry me off, to send me far away from Scotland so I'd never find out."

"He did all of this to secure his place as clan chief?"

"Aye."

Conall pulled Effie back into his arms. "We have time, we'll figure this out together, understand?"

"Together." She smiled.

Bending down, he captured her lips in a feverish kiss.

The rain stopped as Conall's soul settled, and the wind died down to a breeze, yet the clouds remained gray. Long red hair whipped in the air, wrapping around him like soft silk, filling his senses with her sweet honey scent. The woman in his arms was his world, and he would die defending her. He just wished he could have saved her sooner.

Effie's body went limp in his arms. He broke the kiss as she slipped deeper into his embrace. She looked at him confused, as her brows furrowed in pain. "Conall?"

Slipping his hands around her body and holding her up, his hand grazed a hard object protruding from her back. Her dress was wet, and when he pulled his hand away, it was covered in blood. "Effie, nay!" Conall dropped to the ground with Effie in his arms. She had been stabbed.

Tavish laughed and coughed up blood. "She deserves to die." With one last breath, Tavish pushed the dirk deeper into Effie's back.

Gently, Conall laid Effie down on her side and strode over to Tavish, ready to strike a fatal blow. He grabbed the bastard by his neck until he was hanging in the air. "I will take great pleasure in killing ye for everything ye put yer sister through. Rot in hell, forever." Conall squeezed him so hard, his back cracked and his eyes bulged out of their sockets. When he felt Tavish's body jerk a last time, he dropped his limp body on the ground.

Effie coughed, bringing Conall's attention back to her. He ran to her and scooped her up, cradling her in his arms. "Effie, stay with me."

At that moment, James and Rory flew in, hitting the ground in human form.

"Conall, what happened and who's this?" James pointed to Caden.

Caden growled at the rude tone of James's voice.

"I dinnae have time to answer. Effie is wounded and I'm losing her," Conall said.

James walked over and stood behind Conall, assessing the severity of Effie's condition. "The lass needs to see Abigale. And fast."

"Aye."

"And whatever ye do, do not remove that blade until me wife has seen her. If anyone can heal her, it's Abigale."

Conall laid Effie back down. Time was of the essence, he had to shift and make it back to Black Stone in record time. As Conall shifted, the three Dragonkine warriors looked down upon Conall's fallen mate and their hearts ached for their brother.

Careful not to inflict more pain than she was already in, Conall lifted Effie up in his talons and drew her to his chest. He hoped that she would make it through the flight home.

"Conall." She swallowed hard.

"Dinnae talk, me sweet. I'm taking ye home to see Abigale," Conall said through mind-speak.

"Maggie, I can no' leave Maggie behind," she replied. "She's in a bedchamber above the gatehouse."

"Caden, find Maggie and bring her to Black Stone," Conall demanded.

"Aye," Caden said.

James crossed his arms across his chest. "We'll wait here for ye. Oh, and ye might want to cover yerself. No need in frightening the lass."

Rory smirked as he threw a pair of trews at Caden.

"God speed, me friend," James said as Conall left the battlements.

Taking to the sky, Conall left his brethren and headed to Black Stone, pleading to the heavens above that they would make it in time. Losing Effie was not an option. "Stay with me, me love."

⁓

Caden blasted himself a thousand times a fool for agreeing to bring Maggie to Black Stone. Then again, he didn't quite remember agreeing to such a task. Nay, what he should have done was kept to the sky and flown his arse far away. Yet his wings found themselves following Conall.

He didn't understand why he felt the pull to help his kind. Perhaps blood ran deep, or mayhap it was honor that drove him to stay with his kind. Nay, he had lost his honor decades ago. Whatever it may be, he was ready to find the lass and there was no going back.

Dodging and weaving through the crowd, Caden made his way to the gatehouse in a chamber. As he ran across the battlements, he met a group of men who were either drunk or feeling a wee bit too brave. They advanced on Caden, snarling and seething with their swords jabbing at him, telling him that he could not pass. Caden rolled his eyes. Did these men really think they were going to kill him?

Looking down from the battlements, he noticed that the lower balcony was less occupied. Caden took a few more steps back, giving him more distance between himself and the fools in front of him. In a flash, Caden hopped up on the battlement wall and jumped off, landing with a thud on the lower balcony. As the men peered down wondering where their enemy had gone, the blond warrior looked up and shot them the finger, expressing how much he had enjoyed their time together.

With great speed, Caden took off down the long corridor until he reached a window. Needing to get away from the chaos surrounding him, he thought it to be a good idea to hide. Quickly, he slipped in through the window, falling to the ground.

Regaining his feet, he dusted his trews off and finally was able to take a breath, when a pitcher flew across the room and bashed him in the head.

"What the hell!" Caden yelled and felt the urge to rip the fool's head off for hitting him.

"Get out, or I swear, I'll scream!"

He turned and scowled. The air seized in his lungs and he forgot about wanting to harm anyone. The lass in the bed had a candlestick in her hands. She was warning him not to come any closer.

"Ye be Maggie?"

"Why do ye want to know?" God's teeth, the softness of her voice washed over him like a cool morning breeze.

"Effie sent me. I'm here to bring ye to Black Stone." Somehow his feet were moving of their own accord. He reached the lass's bedside.

"I will no' go." The lass crossed her arms over her chest and winced as if she was in pain.

"I'm sorry, but ye have no choice, nor do we have time to argue about it."

Caden was bending over to scoop Maggie up when a bony knee connected with his sacred parts.

"Christ, woman!" Caden backed away. Bent over, he held his ballocks.

"I warned ye to stay away."

For a moment he rested his hands on his knees until the throbbing ceased and the bile settled in his gut.

Looking up at the lass, he smiled. Maggie was a fighter and feisty. He liked that, but alas, this only made the task more difficult than it should be. Why had he gotten himself involved? He should have flown off as soon as the opportunity allowed. Too late now.

Slowly, with his hands up in surrender, he approached the lass. "I'm no' here to hurt ye. I promise."

"How do I know I can trust ye? I dinnae even know ye," Maggie said.

"Here." He extended his hand. "We'll start over. Me name is Caden."

Hesitantly, she held her hand out. "Maggie."

Caden smiled and took her shaking hand in his. "I'm sorry to have to do this, but ye leave me no choice." Before Maggie could pull away, Caden unleashed his sleep magic and the lass went limp and fell back into the bed before she had a chance to protest.

Holding her close as he picked her up, Caden was in more trouble than he could have ever known. This raven-haired lass was exquisite.

18

Abigale jumped out of her seat as Conall busted through the door of Black Stone as if he was breaking into the enemy's stronghold. He held Effie in his arms as he called out for help. Blood soaked her dress.

"Abigale!" James called out. "Where are ye, lass?"

Abigale raced to her husband. "I'm right here."

Horror consumed her when she saw a dagger lodged into Effie's body. "What happened?" She began to examine her. "Oh, merciful heavens!"

Wrapping his plaid around his waist, James met Abigale. "Love, I'll explain everything as soon as I can, but right now, Effie needs ye."

"Please, Abigale, ye must save her," Conall pleaded.

"Of course, Conall. Ye know I'll do everything in me power to save her." Abigale placed her hand on Conall's arm.

"Alice!" Abigale called out.

Alice came rushing from the kitchens. "Lady Abigale." She grew silent as she eyed Effie. "No'!" She clutched Effie's arm.

Abigale placed her hand on Alice's shoulder. "I need ye to be strong, Alice. If I'm going to help her, I'll need ye."

"Aye, my lady."

"Bring me supplies to the upstairs bedchamber. Hurry!" Abigale commanded. "Conall, take Effie to her bedchamber, I'll be right behind ye."

Abigale moved out of the way, for Conall was going to knock down anything or anyone who got in his way.

"And the other woman?" Abigale pointed to the unknown Highlander holding a woman.

"I put her under sleep magic, but she seems to be in pain," the warrior said.

"Rory, help find her a bedchamber and I will be there as soon as I can," Abigale called over her shoulder as she climbed the stairs behind Conall.

"Aye," Rory confirmed and led Caden down a long corridor past the kitchen.

"Ye never cease to amaze me, my beautiful angel," James said as he followed her up the stairs.

"What?" She faced her husband.

"Ye stay so calm and know exactly what to do."

"'Tis just like ye're on the battlefield. Ye know exactly what plan of attack to make to secure victory."

James stared at her swollen belly. "Yet, ye save lives while I take them."

Abigale cupped his face. "James Douglas, ye're the most amazing man I've ever known and ye'll make a fine da. I love ye." She kissed his lips. "Now, Effie needs me. I must hurry." Abigale turned on her heels and quickened her step to Effie's chamber.

The door to the bedchamber was wide open, and Conall had laid Effie on the bed on her stomach. Abigale approached Effie. She was unconscious and her breathing was shallow. Blood stained the back of her dress. "I need that dress off."

*C*onall extended a talon and carefully sliced the fabric away. *God's wounds!* He would have traded places with the lass if he could. The dagger was deep and close to her spine. Being a warrior on the battlefield, he'd seen wounds like this before and the outcome had always been grim.

As Abigale took over, he watched the chamber spin slowly out of focus, words blended into whispered mutters as he broke into a sweat. Conall raked a hand through his mess of hair, blinking and straining to focus. His dragon paced and howled inside him, mourning their mate.

He swayed and lost his balance as his legs buckled. He was going down.

"James!" Abigale called out as she saw Conall staggering. "Conall's passing out!"

With urgency, James crossed the room and grabbed his friend from behind before he hit the ground. "Och, me friend, let's wait outside. Effie's in good hands. And we need to fetch ye some clothes."

"Nay," Conall muttered. "I can no' leave her." He pushed his chief's hands away and swayed.

"Conall, as yer chief and friend, I order ye to leave this room. Ye can come back once Abigale is done. Ye're no' helping Effie by sticking around. Now, let's go."

Damn James for being right. Resisting only put Effie in more danger, that he knew, yet he couldn't convince his body to move. Being weak himself, he needed rest, ale, food, and to walk off this fog inside his head.

"Aye, but I'll be right outside the door."

At that moment, Alice strode in with her arms loaded with cloth and Abigale's herbs, while Rory carried the hot water pot. James took Conall outside the chamber.

Before Conall left, he took one last glance at Effie. He had failed again to protect the ones he loved. If she made it through, he would fly them away from all the violence in Scotland. They would just disappear and forever be together as long as she would have him. He would have that secluded home in the countryside, farming and raising wee bairns. Never would he leave her sight again, not for one moment. Effie was his heart, his mate, his twin soul destined to be forever one. Nay, death was not coming for her, he would no' allow it.

As soon as Conall stepped outside, he gripped the railing and hung his head. James clapped a hand on his shoulder and squeezed. Words escaped his brother, but with James, his actions spoke louder and Conall knew his friend, his brother, felt Effie's pain as deeply as he did.

"'Tis unfair." Conall broke down. "I can no' lose her."

James stood next to him. "Aye, I won't say I know how ye feel because we all feel differently when it comes to our mates, yet one fact remains true. Ye'd give yer own life to save her, that I understand." James paused. "Abigale is fighting for Effie, too."

Conall stared at his leader, 'twas good to have his support.

"Ye have to be strong, she needs yer strength."

Conall peered up from the ground. For a man whose words didn't come easy, James couldn't have been more correct. Aye, pulling himself together was exactly what he intended to do. He wiped the tears from his face and squared his shoulders. "Ye're right. Effie is a fighter."

Caden couldn't quite understand why he still lingered in the dimly lit bedchamber. There were many reasons why he should let the lass go while he still had a chance.

He remembered the way Maggie felt pressed up against his body while he carried her from Caerlaverock Castle and then into the sky. His gaze traced down her face to a perfect pert nose and full lips. He wanted to kiss those lips.

He also admired her fearlessness, the way she fought to protect herself against him. It said something about her spirit. And if any woman was given a chance to truly know him, she'd need strength...

Her hair was raven-black and her eyes were the color of the ocean with the slightest sparkle like stars. And her slight form, barely covered by her sheer shift, was much to his liking.

As he dared another look at her face, he caught a glimpse of blistered flesh peeking from the top of her nightdress on her chest.

God's blood! What kind of trouble had the lass gotten herself into to receive such harsh punishment?

Fighting the urge to look further, he pulled the blanket over her body and stepped away from the bed. He thought better than to involve himself with her problems. The lass was the Black Douglas's problem now. No way in hell was he sticking around. After being locked up, he wanted absolute freedom, no ties to anyone or anything.

19

When the bedchamber door opened and Abigale stepped into the passageway looking exhausted and worried, Conall's heartbeat pounded. Should he prepare for the worst outcome?

"Conall, I've done all I can do. I removed the blade and cauterized the wound, but…"

Before she could finish, Conall interrupted, desperate to see Effie. "Can I go in?"

"Not yet. She's still unconscious. Conall, the blade was close to her spine, leaving me to believe she could very well never walk again. I've seen this sort of injury before. I'm no' going to give ye false hope."

"I can heal her." He placed his hand on the door latch, ready to go inside.

"Conall, she's with child."

As if the latch was hot iron, he quickly let go and paused.

"Alice believes she's about three months into the pregnancy."

Three months? Closing his eyes in relief, he sighed. Effie was pregnant with their child. For the briefest moment joy warmed his heart as he thought about that cottage in the countryside, Effie standing at the front door holding their newborn babe.

"Since I do no' have a lot of knowledge of yer kind has there ever been a situation where a Dragonkine has healed a woman while pregnant? What concerns me is that she'll be in a healing sleep and I dinnae know how the babe will fare."

Conall turned to Abigale with a look of defeat written on his face. "I have no knowledge about it. Our kind usually mates with our females, no' humans."

"James? Do ye know?" She looked at her husband.

"Nay, *bele ange*. I dinnae know."

Frustration festered as Conall's hope of saving Effie crumbled. There had to be something he could do. For Christ sake, he was a dragon, there was magic pulsing through his blood. "Ye be telling me that if I heal her, it could harm the babe?"

"Aye."

"And if I dinnae heal her, she'll die?"

Abigale hung her head. "Aye," she choked. "And even if ye heal her, there's still a chance she'll never walk again."

Conall couldn't believe what he was hearing. If he healed his wife, she could lose the babe, or he could do nothing and leave fate in God's hands.

He needed to get his head straight.

Back at Caerlaverock the lass had showed courage beyond compare, even risking her own life to save him. Their fates had turned, and now she needed him to fight for her more than ever.

He knew what he had to do. To hell with fate. If he could save the woman he loved, he would do it and never think twice about it. Without further hesitation, he opened the chamber door. He was going to save Effie and worry about the ramifications later.

The smell of burning sage clung to the air, warding off the evil spirits that might be lurking around Effie's bedchamber. Alice had sworn to Conall that her ritual would help the healing process. Abigale and James's girls made trinkets from a rowan tree and hung them around the bed and placed one around Conall's neck, telling him he, too, needed to be healed.

In the evening, as the Dragonkine brothers, Alice, and Abigale stopped by the bedchamber to pray over Effie, the wee one played a tune on the harp that Effie had taught her. Though Conall wanted to be left alone, he knew everyone else loved Effie, too.

Although he believed it all to be silly folklore, he accepted the gifts and enjoyed the company. Perhaps putting a wee bit of faith in those treasures wasn't a bad idea after all. All he had left was hope as the second day of the healing was coming to an end.

Alice had brought food up to him and by the second trip, she had a bath prepared and clean clothes laid out. Guilty didn't come close to describing how he felt for leaving her side when Alice persisted that he take a bath and eat to keep his strength up. Being back home, the evil magic he'd once felt was long gone and his own wounds were healed, which made him feel even guiltier. He was healed while his love was still wounded.

Even though Effie felt no pain and slept peacefully, alas he couldn't shake the guilt-ridden feeling. He spent the days washing the blood from her body, brushing her beautiful red hair, and tending to the fire in the hearth, making sure she was comfortable.

Now Conall sat in a chair next to Effie reflecting on how his life, his long never-ending life, had come full circle. He had been here before, had seen the aftermath of violence that was brought upon his family. Coming home from hunting to find his wife and son burned and their house in flames. He hated himself more than the rogue Vikings who had left him hollow and took away his life, his family. He'd failed to protect them. And, as if fate wasn't enough of a bloody bastard, he was in the same situation all over again with Effie, except this time he had hope. There had been no hope for his first wife and son.

Aye, he had hope. He had put Effie under a healing sleep regardless of the risk to their unborn babe.

Conall stood and walked over to Effie. His gaze moved up her body and settled on her stomach. Even though she wasn't showing, there was a wee babe in there fighting for its life. He placed his hand flat on her stomach. "Please forgive me, wee one." His voice was raspy and low. "Yer mum and I need ye to be strong and brave." He kissed her belly.

As soon as he made contact with Effie, he dropped to his knees. Sorrow washed over him in violent waves, he couldn't stop the tears. "Stay with me," he said between deep breaths as he clenched the furs on the bed. "I can no' lose ye, lass."

Blinking past the tears, he pressed his head against her chest and listened to her breathe. The rhythmic beating of her heart soothed him and his dragon, confirming that she was indeed still with him and fighting.

He rubbed her stomach in a circular motion.

"Conall," she whispered.

He raised his head and was beyond belief when forest-green eyes stared back at him. "Effie? Ye're awake?"

Coughing, she said, "Aye."

Conall stood and threw his arms around her, nuzzling her neck. "Thank the gods!"

"Conall, ye're...squishing me."

Regaining his composure, he straightened, never taking his hands off her. "Forgive me. I thought I'd lost ye, lass."

"Nay," she coughed again. "I'm here."

Cursing himself a fool, he let go of her hand and fetched her some water. "Here, drink this." He sat back down and continued to rub his hands up and down her arms. "Do ye remember what happened?"

Effie paused from drinking. Her eyes grew big. "I was falling and you caught me."

"Aye, I did."

"And I killed Tavish." She frowned. "Then I must have fainted. I dinnae remember anything after that." There was a hint of panic in her tone. Conall could see that she was trying to make sense of it all.

"Effie, yer brother wasn't dead. I flew ye back to the tower and as I was making sure ye were all right, he stabbed yer back with a dagger."

"But I stabbed him."

"Aye, I couldn't believe it meself. But the bastard had one last fight in him and then I finished him off."

"I see."

"I didnae know what else to do, so I flew ye back here so Abigale could heal ye, but..." He raked a hand through his hair. "Ye lost a lot of blood, lass, and under the circumstances, I had to heal ye for if not I would have lost ye."

"What do ye mean, circumstances?" She struggled to sit up. Helping her, Conall lifted her until her back rested comfortably on an array of pillows behind her.

"Do ye need anything, like food? Aye, ye must be hungry."

"Dinnae change the subject, Conall. There's something ye're no' telling me. Why can I no' feel me legs?"

She had to know he'd healed her in order to save her life. And to add to her problems she might never walk again. Hating the fact he had to be the bearer of bad news, Conall gave pause to gather up his thoughts.

"Effie." He sat down with her slender hand in his. "I do no' know where to start." He took a deep breath and hoped she would understand his motives were out of love for her.

Her brows creased.

"The dagger was embedded close to yer spine. Ye can no' feel yer legs because of the severity of yer wound. Abigale did all that she could, but she needed me help. Even with me magic there is no guarantee ye will walk again."

"So, are ye telling me I'll never walk?"

"'Tis possible, aye. We'll only know as ye fully heal."

Effie stilled as she wadded the sheet in her hands. Conall knew it was a lot for the lass to process, but he needed to tell her everything. "Effie, ye're with child."

"A babe?"

Conall smiled, for he couldn't help it. The thought of Effie carrying his child left him proud and warm inside. Even his dragon purred at that idea. "But—"

"Oh, please, Conall, how much worse can it be? Dinnae tell me the babe is at risk."

As quickly as his joy at her waking had come, his insides turned sorrowful. Fate had really kicked him hard in the ballocks. Conall blew out a deep breath. "I had to make a decision, and I hope in time ye can forgive me. Abigale warned me that if I healed ye, the babe might not make it. We dinnae know how the babe will react to me magic. I had to save ye, me sweet. I know it was a selfish act, but I can no' live without ye."

Effie remained silent a little longer than Conall would have liked. He was ready for her to kick his arse out of the chamber for putting their babe at risk. Furthermore, he wouldn't blame her if she did.

"Conall, there's nothing to forgive. Ye did the best ye could to save me..." She reached over and squeezed his arm. "And ye did. I'm alive because of ye. Our babe will be fine."

He leaned in, giving her a soft kiss. "I love ye, lass, and whatever may be, I'll be here." His words were more than a promise, they were an assurance.

Her smile was all he needed as he looked down at his beautiful red-haired lass. It reassured him that he'd done right by her. Together they would overcome their situation, and no matter what, he'd be by her side.

"Conall, can ye bring me some food?"

"Aye, what do ye fancy?"

"Alice's special oat cakes."

Bending down, he kissed her forehead and lingered for a brief moment as he closed his eyes and thanked the gods his Effie was alive and he was forgiven.

20

The candlestick bounced off Effie's bedchamber door and fell onto the floor as Conall slammed the door shut. Tears streamed down her face as she realized she'd thrown it at him in a frustrated rage over their wedding ceremony.

Walking to her husband on their wedding day was all she'd thought about, until Tavish had taken that dream away. She wanted to cancel the ceremony, but Conall refused. He wanted to marry her as soon as possible. However, she wasn't ready to face the world confined to a chair.

Effie was losing hope that she'd ever be able to walk again. A long fortnight had passed and Effie was no closer to being able to walk again. Hope was fading…fast.

Conall had done everything in his power to heal her. He massaged her legs with healing oils that Abigale swore by, yet no luck. He tried to take her outside for fresh air and bring her to the great hall for meals, but she refused. She didn't want to be a burden nor to be pitied.

Irritated, she huffed and threw her body back down onto the bed, heaving a pillow across the room. There were so many damn pillows. As she lay, she blew a loose curl from her face, ashamed of how she'd treated Conall. It was unforgivable. He was only trying to help her, which only made her feel worse.

Perhaps it was the sage wafting in the air that was driving her daft or the way the trinkets would rattle as the wind blew in from the open window. Nay, there was one thing driving her mad. Her legs. Her legs would just not move.

She turned toward the nightstand. A rolled piece of parchment was on the table. Sir Neil had brought her a missive that had been addressed to her when he'd visited. He'd found it in her father's solar.

Scooting toward the side of the bed, she opened the missive.

She read her father's last words.

Dearest daughter,

It saddens me heart that we have drifted apart, yet I knew the time would come when ye would blossom into a beautiful bird and leave the nest. Ye're strong just like yer mother. I still miss her dearly. Ye remind me of her, ye have her smile and courage. She'd be proud of ye just as I am.

I know I've made mistakes in the past, I strayed from yer mother and caused her pain. I should have told ye sooner, but Tavish is me bastard. I never loved his mother, and I think Tavish knew this and hated me for it. His hatred grew when ye were born. He felt threatened by ye because pure Maxwell blood runs through yer veins and heart.

Ye're probably asking yerself why I didnae tell ye sooner. Perhaps I wanted to protect ye from all the politics of being a clan chief. Whatever it may have been me dearest, ye are the one and only true Maxwell and the only one to take me place.

Keep Sir Neil close. He will protect ye. As for I... och lass, I dinnae need to tell ye what ye already know. I'm with yer mother and I will tell her what a fine lass ye've become.

Da

Tears streamed down her cheeks.

"Oh da, I wish I could have said goodbye." She sniffed and wiped her face with the back of her hands. If only she could have seen him one last time.

Her father was a strong leader. How was she going to follow in her father's footsteps when she couldn't walk? How would she ride out in battle to encourage her warriors to fight for her and their clan? Her clan would be an easy target in the future. There were few female chieftains, especially crippled ones.

Without a doubt, Neil would stand by her. He'd proven his loyalty, and she could count on him to advise her. He was just like a father and she needed him more than ever.

Another thought came to her as she rubbed her belly. A babe. She had to believe some good could come out of the disaster she and Conall had been through. It broke her heart knowing that Conall would never forgive himself if the babe didn't make it.

So, she had only one option; she needed to walk. She needed to be strong for Conall, the babe, and her clan. There were too many people depending on her. Her mother fought her illness to the death, her father fought to his last breath, and she'd been fighting her whole life to free herself from a horrific past. There was no honor in lying down like a defeated coward. If her family had taught her one thing, it was to fight.

Determined more than ever, she ripped the blankets off and rose up on her elbows. Glaring at her toes, she dared them to disobey. "Move ye bloody bastards. Wiggle." With determination, she stared at her feet. Her eyes grew wide as she felt a light prickling sensation in her big toe. *Aye*, there was hope.

As her feet became more accustomed to the movement, the prickling sensation moved up her calf and caused her muscles to twitch.

Once she was comfortable with moving her toes, she focused on her ankles. Feeling had slowly crept into her feet and up her legs. With great concentration, she managed to rotate her ankles. But the effort exhausted her. She fell back against the pillows and took a deep breath. Fighting the urge to give up, she tried again, moving her legs.

That's when she felt a distant flutter in her stomach. Effie placed her hand over her belly and smiled. "Me babe."

She sat up. "The babe. I must tell Conall." As if she had forgotten about her useless legs, she heaved them over to the side of the bed and touched her toes to the stone floor. The coldness of the ground sent a welcoming shiver over her skin. *Aye,* she thought, *'tis a good sign.*

⁓

After the morning meal was finished, James called the Dragonkine warriors to a meeting. Kine business had been set aside until Effie's condition was stable, and Conall was grateful. Effie and the babe were the only things running through his mind.

James met Conall as they both walked up the stairs to the solar.

"So, Conall." James clasped a hand on his best friend's shoulder. "I heard a crash coming from Effie's chamber this morn as me and Abigale were walking to break our fast. Is Effie well?" He sounded as if he was deeply concerned, but there was a hint of mischief in James's words.

Conall blew out a breath. "Aye, if ye call being able to throw a candlestick part of her recovery. She does no' like me opinion on our wedding plans."

"I see. Perhaps ye need to give the lass some more time to heal before talking about a wedding."

"Aye, I just want her to know I love her, and no matter what the outcome is, I will be there for her."

James stopped right outside the doors and turned to his friend. "Me brother, have no doubt. The lass loves ye. And the two of ye are home and safe."

And that he was, home with his red-haired lass and his brothers.

Conall grew serious. His friend had risked their secrecy to rescue him. That's what Dragonkine warriors did. Loyalty ran more than scale-deep, it was embedded in their souls.

"James, thank ye for coming to me aid. I know it was no easy decision to make, putting the Kine at risk."

"Ye'd do the same for me."

As they walked into the room, Magnus, Rory, and Caden greeted them. James took his seat behind the big wooden desk in the center of the room while Conall took his usual spot next to the hearth.

As the meeting started, Conall explained what had happened back at Caerlaverock Castle, how Tavish had ambushed him and his men. Also, how Tavish had blamed the English attack on Clan Douglas.

"I didnae realize how close we were to a clan war." James rubbed his chin.

"Aye." Conall shook his head at the thought. "I need to inform Broc's family about what happened."

Sadness filled his heart; Broc's family would be devastated to learn of their son's death. Broc was a good lad, the finest.

"No need. Broc is here and recovering, thanks to me wife. He was the one who informed us ye were in trouble."

Stunned, Conall couldn't believe the lad had survived. "Abigale is a guardian angel."

James smiled proudly.

The dark cloud returned over Conall as he recalled the deadly black magic in the dungeon.

"James, there was black magic in that place, a spell so strong it trapped me dragon. I was unable to heal and I could no' shift."

The other warriors were suddenly interested in everything he had to say.

"Like that same dark magic that almost killed me?" James asked.

"Aye, it must be."

"Och, laddies, it seems Marcus must be up to no good," Magnus said.

James looked around the room. "Nay, I dinnae think it was Marcus this time. When I went back to bury Tavish, his body was gone."

"Aye," Rory said. "But someone else could have buried the bastard."

"Nay, it's the blood trail I saw leaving the tower that concerns me and might answer our question about the magic. The trail began with human footprints, then morphed into a webbed print. But what concerns me more is that it looked as if a tail was dragged through the blood." James finished.

"It can no' be." Conall stood and paced in front of the hearth. "I broke the bastard's neck with me own bare hands."

"I believe James. Tavish is more than what we think he is, and now he's on the loose," Magnus said.

"Caden, ye were in that dungeon longer than me, what say ye?" Conall questioned.

Caden stood with his arms crossed over his chest. "Ye're right. It's black magic that ye felt in the cell. How it got there, I do no' know."

"And how did ye end up imprisoned at Caerlaverock?" James inquired.

Caden turned back to the window and pulled his cloak up around his shoulders. He seemed to care naught about the situation. The only reason he stayed at Black Stone was because he'd been ordered to.

Rory advanced on Caden, throwing him up against the wall. "I do believe ye were asked a question."

Caden glared at him.

Conall stepped between the two dragons. "Stand down, Rory. Caden is one of us. He can be trusted."

Rory eased his grip on Caden but got in one last word before he sat back down. "I'll be watching ye."

"Conall?" James raised a brow in question.

"He didnae tell me much, just that he was imprisoned for who he was." Conall looked over at Caden and nodded.

"So Tavish knew ye were Dragonkine?" James asked.

Caden shrugged his shoulders.

"Laddie, it would fare ye well no' to anger the Black Douglas," Magnus warned.

Again, Caden shrugged, making it perfectly clear he cared not.

As the meeting carried on, James informed Conall they needed to build an army and form a plan of attack against Marcus and the ancients. But the problem was they needed more Kine.

The best strategy was keeping their interests west to the holy ground of Govan. That's where Drest had been laid to rest, and that's where Marcus would make his way first.

There were four clans near Govan. Which one Marcus would attack first was anyone's guess.

Magnus, Conall, and James reviewed a map of the holy ground.

"If I were planning to attack," James offered, "I would head north." He pointed at the map. "Take out the smallest clan first."

"Aye," Magnus concurred.

"We need to send word about a possible attack. Warn their people and offer our protection," James said.

Rory stepped beside James and Conall. "And how do ye suppose we do that? Tell them about the dragon ancients coming for them? Ye saw how well Dumfries took to our dragons. I'm surprised we dinnae have dragon slayers burning down our home." Rory said.

"Och, we're dragons, Guardians of Scotland, regardless of what the people think. If we do no' stop this awakening, we're all dead. I love me wife too much to lose her. I will do whatever it takes to protect her." James's words never rang truer.

Being the master strategist, James advanced his plan of attack as he further examined the map. "Four clans surround the holy ground here." He placed a dragonhead figurine down on the auld kingdom of Govan. "Lanarkshire to the south, which is me brother, Archie's land." He placed another dragonhead on the map. "We'll have that secured in no time. To the east lies Helmfirth." Another piece marked the spot.

"To the west, Renfrewshire. To the north, Ravenloch, there's a small clan there. This will be a challenge. They do no' trust easily." He paused. "If we place a Kine in each one of these sites, we can secure the borders of Govan and prevent Marcus from unleashing hell on Scotland."

James stood straight and looked at his men. "Who's with me?"

Without hesitation, Magnus answered, "Aye, laddie."

Rory paused and looked at the map, then back at James. "Aye, me brother."

And before Conall could answer, Caden strode over to the table and grabbed the dragonhead piece off the area of Ravenloch. "I'm in."

Together, they could not fail.

21

Like a newborn fawn trying to walk for the first time, Effie stood on weak, shaky legs. The pin-prick sensations that shot up her feet and legs reminded her of when her legs would fall asleep. She dared to take a step. "'Tis no' so bad," she reassured herself.

Sweat beaded across her forehead as she concentrated on moving her other leg. If only it would move. With faith and stubborn determination, her leg moved.

"Och." Squaring her shoulders, she blew a red tendril of hair from her face. "The first step is no' so bad."

She shuffled another step and the prickling needles faded into a dull pain.

A loud knock at her door startled her and broke her concentration, making her legs buckle. Within two long strides, Conall raced across the threshold, catching Effie by the waist before she sank to the ground. He pulled her onto his lap as they sat on the bed.

"What were ye thinking, lass?"

Pulling from his embrace, she looked excitedly into his gray eyes. "I felt the babe, Conall." She smiled as tears welled in her eyes.

"Are ye sure?" Conall asked with just as much excitement.

"Aye. I had to come and tell ye. I took two steps before ye came in."

"Two steps?" he said adoringly as he wiped a tear away from her face.

"Two."

He reached out to touch her stomach. "May I?"

"Conall, dinnae be silly, of course." She grabbed his hand and placed it right where she felt the flutters. "The last time I felt the babe move was right here."

As soon as she felt his hand on her skin, a wave of pure desire whirled up inside her. She might have lost some feeling in her legs, but there was no doubt she could feel Conall igniting her passion.

Conall bent his head down to talk to the wee babe. "Yer mum is brave and strong, aye?" Conall rubbed her belly. "Ye be just like her."

Effie kissed the top of his head. "Ye'll be a great Da."

"Aye, I'll always be by yer side, me sweet."

"I have no doubt."

Conall stood and gathered Effie into his arms. He walked to the side of the bed and laid her down, climbing in next to her. He held her in a tight embrace. "Promise me the next time ye go testing yer legs, ye'll let me know first."

"I promise." Effie looked up. This man was her everything, her protector, her lover, her savior, her dragon. Just as he would have moved heaven and earth to be with her, she would do the same for him. Her love for him was like nothing she had ever experienced and now she was going to be the mother of his child. Her heart warmed as she lay there in awe of her Highlander. "I love ye, Conall Hamilton." She kissed his lips.

"And I ye, Effie Maxwell."

"Och, that would be Laird Maxwell," she teased.

Conall's face grew grim. It was unusual for a woman to hold such power. She worried Conall wouldn't accept her new position. "Ye dinnae like the idea of me being a laird?"

"No."

Effie pulled away and sat up. "I knew it. Ye dinnae like to see a woman in power."

"'Tis no' that. Dinnae be daft." Conall pulled her back into his arms. "With that power comes danger. I almost lost ye once and it about killed me. I can no' lose ye. Dark times have fallen upon us. James has a plan to rid Scotland of evil and protect our loved ones, but it will come at a great cost. People will die." Conall looked down at her and tipped her chin up until she looked him in the eyes. "I promise as long as I live, ye'll be safe."

Effie caressed his cheek. "I know yer heart. And I know with a dragon by me side we can beat this evil." Conall kissed her gently on the lips. Effie deepened the kiss. She slid her hands down his broad shoulders to his well-defined back until she reached the end of his tunic. Tugging it up his torso, Conall broke their kiss long enough to shed his shirt.

"Are ye sure?" Conall asked.

Effie nodded. "I've missed ye."

A quivering thrill ran down her spine as she felt the roughness of his hands skim over her body and remove her shift. "Ye're a bonny lass." He gazed at her body as if he was deciding where to start devouring first.

By the saints, she loved her dragon.

22

𝓔ffie paused outside of Maggie's bedchamber door, her hand balled in a fist ready to knock. Facing Maggie for the first time since Tavish's assault had kept Effie up all night. She'd couldn't stop blaming herself. This had been all her fault. She was supposed to have protected Maggie, instead she allowed the wolf to devour her.

Effie closed her eyes and took in a deep breath before she knocked on the door. No one answered, however she knew Maggie was in there. She hadn't left the bedchamber since she arrived at Black Stone.

"Maggie, 'tis me. I'm coming in."

Effie opened the door and wasn't surprised when Maggie didn't acknowledge her.

"Abigale made some healing lotion for ye." Effie reached inside her velvet bag that hung on her waist and pulled out a small bottle of lotion. "I can help ye apply it if ye would like."

"Ye've done enough," Maggie replied as she stared at the ceiling.

"I'm so sorry." Effie began to sit next to Maggie on the bed.

"Nay, dinnae bother making yerself comfortable. Ye will no' be staying."

"How can I make it right?"

Maggie faced Effie. Tears rolled from her eyes. "There is nothing ye can do. Ye promised to protect me from him."

"I know, and I will never forgive meself for letting him harm ye."

"Ye're a liar. Ye did this to me." Maggie rolled over turning her back on Effie.

"Please, Maggie. I—"

"Get out!"

Effie hung her head. Her heart ached.

Effie quit the bedchamber. As she left, she saw a glimpse of the blond warrior who'd brought Maggie to the castle turn down the corridor. "Excuse me," she called out and ran to catch-up with him. As she reached the end of the corridor he'd disappeared.

Where had he gone? She thought it was strange for him to be outside Maggie's chamber.

"There ye are."

She looked behind her and to her relief she saw Conall walking toward her. As Conall reached her, he bent down and kissed her. "I've been looking for ye. Where have ye been? Breakfast is ready."

"I'm sorry. I went to check on Maggie."

"How is she?"

"Not good. She's in a lot of pain." Effie looked away, not wanting to tell him that Maggie hated her.

Conall lifted her chin with his figure, making her look at him. "And..."

"Conall, she blames me for what Tavish did to her and I dinnae blame her."

"Ye're being too hard on yerself. Ye brought her here to make sure she receives the care she needs and to heal from her burns. She should be grateful."

Effie shook her head and started down the corridor. "Nay, she has every right to hate me. I failed her."

Conall grabbed her arm and she turned to face him. "Effie, there was no way of knowing that Tavish was going to hurt Maggie. Give her some time to heal physically and emotionally. I promise ye in time she'll forgive ye."

"I hope that ye're right, for Maggie's sake. She should no' have to bear all of this on her own. I want to be here for her."

"I know and ye will." Conall tucked a strand of her hair behind her ear, the small loving gesture made her heart warm. This man, dragon, truly loved her, and at this moment she needed to feel loved. "Now, lets get ye two fed." He looked down at her belly.

"Aye," she smiled. "We're hungry."

Reaching the top of the stairs, she paused as she looked down into the great hall. Her heart warmed at the sight of her friends sitting together at the long table. They were her family. Abigale and James at the head of the table appeared as if they were in their own world. James fed his wife fresh fruit and kissed her. Abigale giggled in delight.

Rory and Magnus jested back and forth about a lass Rory had bedded the night before. She couldn't quite make out what they were saying. Something along the line of questioning the lass's easy virtue and how much mead was involved. It must have been in poor taste because Alice shook her head at the Highlanders and clucked her tongue.

A smaller table across from the larger one was filled with children. Flora and Annis sat side by side eating their breakfast when a hunk of bread flew past Flora coming from Neven's direction. The bread landed in Flora's bowl, splattering porridge onto the front of her dress. Flora jumped out of her seat.

In retaliation, Annis stuck her tongue out at Neven, but he just laughed. "Do no' worry, Annis." She scowled at the lad as she cleaned her dress off. "One day, he'll be sorry that he picked on me."

"Good morn, sleeping beauty," Alice joked.

"Aye, I overslept." Effie gave Conall a knowing a smile as he led her to the table where she sat between him and Abigale.

"Ye look stunning this morn, Effie. The extra rest did ye good. Mayhap I should have overslept." Abigale elbowed her husband in the ribs.

"Och, lass. What do ye mean, sleep? I've no' slept a wink in the past month. Ye two take up half the bed." He looked down at her belly, then back to her face where he met a stern expression.

Abigale gave him another jab in the ribs as James kissed her cheek. "Ye're lucky I love ye, James Douglas." She smiled.

Conall leaned into Effie and whispered in her ear. "I'll start making us a bigger bed right away," he jested.

Effie laughed.

"How are ye feeling? Better, aye?" Abigale asked Effie.

"Oh, much better. Life couldn't be better." Effie winked at Conall as he piled fruit, bread, and cheese onto her trencher.

"He was so worried about ye. Conall's a good man and he loves ye verra much," Abigale said.

"Aye, and I love him. Abigale, there was a time back at Caerlaverock that I thought I would never see him again and…"

"Dinna fash yerself." Abigale placed a reassuring hand on Effie's arm. "'Tis in the past. All that matters is now."

Indeed, the past was over. Quite frankly, she wished she didn't have to go back to Caerlaverock, ever. But she was chief now. Eventually she would have to return. Sir Neil was to act as clan chief until her return; Caerlaverock castle was in good hands. It was too soon to relive the hell she and Conall had gone through. Plus, her home was here at Black Stone on the Hill with clan Douglas. She wanted to raise her family in Angus.

"How's Maggie this morn?" Abigale asked.

"She's still in a lot of pain," Effie answered and averted her gaze to her trencher, praying Abigle wouldn't ask any more questions. She couldn't bear to tell her best friend that Tavish, her brother, had caused Maggie this pain

Leaning forward, Abigale changed the subject. "And ye have a wedding coming up," she beamed. "Do ye have time after we eat to discuss the girls' dresses? Alice has been working on Annis's dress and the wee one has been a bit stubborn about it."

Popping a piece of bread in her mouth, Effie replied, "Aye, that would be fun. Annis and I get along verra well. We'll have a talk." She winked.

"Verra well then. I'll go and help Alice clean up until ye're done eating." Abigale rose from her seat and started to collect the nearby trenchers when she doubled over, clenching her belly. Pain creased her face. "Oww!"

James shot out of his chair and wrapped his arm around her shoulders. "Abigale, what's wrong?"

"'Tis the babe," she said through clenched teeth.

"The babe?" James replied, shocked.

Alice calmly left her seat and walked to the head of the table where Abigale was bent over. "James, yer wife is in labor. I'll take it from here." She placed her hand on James's arm to reassure him that his wife was all right.

James stood firm with his arm protectively around Abigale. "Nay, I'm staying with her. I will no' leave. I can use me magic to help with the pain... I can put her to sleep." James used every excuse to stay with his wife.

"Nay, she must be awake in order to push."

"To push?"

"How else is she going to deliver the babe? Must I remind ye, James Douglas, that I've birthed me share of babes including ye and yer brother. I'm the best midwife ye have. Now step aside and let me take care of Lady Abigale."

Although he'd thought he was prepared for the birth of their child, fear had brought out a different side of him. Of course, she had to push the babe out! But he was used to being in control. The babe was in control now.

Abigale screamed again and banged her fist on the table "James!" She breathed rapidly. "The babe is coming."

The look of desperation in her blue eyes should have been enough warning to make his arse move and allow Alice to take over; however, he still refused to leave his wife.

Conall stood next to his friend and squeezed his shoulder. "Brother, Abigale needs yer strength and understanding right now. Let Alice see to her."

"Conall is right," Effie added. "Ye dinnae want to put the babe in danger. Alice is the best and I'll be there, too. I give ye me word."

Hesitantly, James let go of his wife.

Alice nodded, then said, "Effie, fetch me blankets and make sure there's a fire in the hearth for hot water."

"Aye." Effie hurried off.

"Conall, Rory, and Magnus, ye make damn sure James stays out of their bedchamber. We're going to have a babe soon."

Alice guided and supported Abigale up the stairs and into her bedchamber. All the while, James was left defenseless. As the women left his sight, it hit him like a sack of rocks; his child was on its way into the world. He dinnae like being an outsider. He should be in that damn room comforting his wife.

23

The morning hours gave way to afternoon and still no babe. Long into the night, James sat in front of the hearth in the great hall, staring intently at the raging flames. He desperately wanted to be with his wife.

The agonizing cries of pain and desperate pleas to God from Abigale were increasing by the hour and tried his resolve to keep his arse planted in the chair. The louder she was, the more difficult it became to keep his composure. He was pulled tight, ready to snap.

Dragonkine filled the great hall. He felt their watchful gazes. Magnus sat next to him, keeping a firm eye on him while sharpening his battle axe. Rory sat at the table peering over a roasted leg of lamb, waiting to for him to make a move. And Conall, the dragon who knew him best, was posted at the base of the stairs. By Conall's stance, he knew it was only a matter of time before he'd have to hold James back.

"Blessed Mary!" Abigale yelled, sending the pain straight to James's heart. Closing his eyes, he tapped his foot on the floor. His nerves were unraveling. If only he could take her pain away.

After another scream, he lost control. He shot out of the chair, sending the damn thing crashing behind him. His black cloak fell to the floor as he rushed to the stairs, only to be held back by his trusted friend.

"Conall, damn it! Let me pass!" He struggled against Conall's hold.

"I can no' let ye do that."

"I'm in no condition to be responsible for me actions. I'll only ask ye one more time. Let. Me. Pass," James demanded through gritted teeth.

"Nay, Alice will have me arse for it."

With one fluid motion, James swung his arm at Conall's head. Conall ducked just in time, and James's fist hit the stone wall. Stone and mortar crumbled, leaving behind a huge hole.

"Bastard! Ye were going to hit me!" Conall said.

"And I'll do it again if ye dinnae let me pass," James snarled. His eyes swirled amber and his pupils transformed to reptilian slits. It was no surprise, James was going to go dragon if the men couldn't talk some sense into him.

Rory grabbed James from behind, holding his arms.

Magnus flew out of his seat and raced to Conall's side. Getting past two dragons... Now that would be a challenge.

Rory growled, "Let it go, James. Abigale has enough to deal with, she does no' need yer pigheadedness!"

"Rory, if ye do no' let me go, so help me..."

Just then, another bloodcurdling scream came.

"Aaaahhhh!"

"Abigale, push!" Alice yelled.

The Highlanders, who knew no weakness, who stared death in its ugly face, froze. James shrugged out of Rory's hold as they all stared in complete horror at the top of the stairs.

Silence sliced the air for what seemed like an eternity. The screaming had stopped suddenly.

What the hell was going on? James knew his wife was having their babe, but the antagonizing quietness after hours of desperate wailing had him thinking something had gone terribly wrong. *Come on, Abigale, scream out, say something so I know ye are well.*

As if someone was listening from above, the tiniest cry echoed through the quietness and slammed into James's chest. The warrior stood stoic. His child had been born.

The Highlanders looked at one another, smiling.

Like his arse was on fire, James took the stairs three at a time. He reached the top, made a sharp right, and ran toward his bedchamber, only to be stopped by Alice.

"Och, I was just fixing to come fetch ye," she said.

James continued to the door, where Alice placed her hand on his arm and stopped him. "James Douglas, look at me."

Slowly, he turned his focus on Alice. His heart suddenly took a nosedive straight into his gut as the worried look on Alice's face gnawed at him. This was when Alice would tell him Abigale hadn't made it, that she died giving birth. He clenched his jaw, preparing for the worst news.

"Abigale had a difficult birth but she fares well. She'll be fine with a wee bit of rest. Now, if ye'll be on yer best behavior, I'll let ye in."

Thank Christ, Abigale was alright. He let out a breath of relief. He was a wreck. One minute he was ready to fight the devil, then the next, he was close to tears.

"Go on." Alice nudged him with her shoulder.

He hugged Alice. "Thank ye."

"Och, ye dinnae have to thank me. Thank yer wife." Alice stepped away and gave James a reassuring smile.

She busied herself down the corridor and called out over her shoulder, "I'll be back in a wee bit to check on the three of ye."

The three of ye? James's heart seized as he paused to open the door.

"Go on," Conall encouraged.

James looked behind him to find his brothers right there, just as eager to meet the wee bairn.

Rory shouldered his way past Conall and Magnus to James. "If ye're no' dragon enough to open the damn door, then I'll do it." Rory went for the door and was pulled back from it by the back of his tunic.

"Over me dead body ye will," James threatened.

The men stepped back as James stepped inside.

The view in front of him was like none he had ever seen. His beautiful wife lay on their bed, propped up by pillows, watching him. Her auburn hair, wet with sweat, stuck around her angelic face. Her blue eyes looked up at his as if she was seeking his approval.

He tried to make his feet move, but the blasted things didn't want to listen.

Effie joined him, holding a bundle swaddled in white linen. It didn't move, nor make a sound. James started to sweat, and panic began to rile up his nerves again.

"My, Laird." Effie nodded toward the bundle in her arms.

James swallowed and took a step back like she'd held the plague in her arms. "I... I..." He looked at Abigale again, unsure what to do.

"James Douglas, dinnae ye want to meet yer daughter?" Abigale asked from across the room.

"A daughter?" James repeated. He had a daughter.

"Aye," Abigale answered.

He stepped closer to Effie. The babe was peacefully sleeping as Effie gently bounced the bundle in her arms. Her eyes were closed and he caught himself wondering what color they might be. He smiled in awe.

"I have to fetch the priest so he can start the baptism," Effie announced and motioned for James to take the babe.

"Nay, I'll go." James sought out any excuse not to hold the babe. Fear overwhelmed him, what if he hurt her? "Ye stay here with Abigale." He wiped the sweat from his brow. "I'll be back."

~

Effie turned to Abigale and watched as tears streamed down her best friend's face. "Oh, Abigale, I be so sorry." She walked over and sat on the bed with the babe in her arms.

Abigale put her head in her hands. "I was afraid of this."

Effie shushed the babe as she squirmed in her arms. "What do ye mean?"

"Oh, Effie, ye know how James is. 'Tis so hard to read that man sometimes." Abigale sniffled and glanced up from her hands and took a deep breath. "I was afraid that the bairn's arrival would drive him daft." Abigale shrugged her shoulders. "Mayhap he wanted a son."

"Nonsense. James loves ye, he'll be back." Effie tried to reassure Abigale, but no words were going to comfort her friend until James returned.

"I'm no' so sure. The Black Douglas side of him is unpredictable."

"But ye have tamed that side" Effie looked down at the bairn. "She is his flesh and blood. He will no' turn her away, nor ye."

"I pray that ye're right." Abigale wiped a tear from her cheek. "James has had a difficult time adjusting to his new life with me. I know how much it means to him to be on the battlefield. He's spent most of his life fighting to regain his lands and family name. Now, because of marrying me, he's bound to keep his oath to me father to protect me. Mayhap I should have stayed at the nunnery."

"Abigale, ye're talking nonsense and I won't hear another pitiful word."

"I'm sorry. I feel so sad when I have nothing to be sad about."

"That's because ye just had a babe. Ye and James need time to heal, together. I promise, he'll be back."

"I hope ye're right."

Effie would make sure she was right even if it meant knocking sense into that suborn dragon. "Abigale let's pray god will give James a swift kick in the arse."

Abigale laughed as Effie handed the babe to her. "Aye, let's pray."

24

Loathing himself for leaving, James made his way to the kirk to fetch the priest. Normally the father and godparents were the ones to bring a newborn to the kirk for the baptism, however, Abigale had been adamant that the babe remain in their bedchamber where it was warm.

He strode with heavy feet out of the great hall and into the cold night air. When he thought about holding that wee one, he'd panicked. Nay, he was scared, pure and simple. "Coward," he spat.

He paused and looked down at his shaking hands. People had died by these hands. He knew what lived inside him; a dragon. "God's blood!" He was unworthy to hold such an innocent babe in his arms.

Fresh air was what he needed. He'd been on edge from the moment Abigale doubled over in pain. Although she had fared well, it was seeing his own flesh and blood that had sent him over the edge. He had refused his daughter.

Aye, a coward. How quickly the wee babe had taken control of the situation, sending him running for the Highlands with his tail tucked between his legs. For Christ sake, he'd been through far worse.

Ashamed for acting like a fool, James quickened his pace, for he felt a strong need pulling him back to his wife and daughter.

A daughter? He stopped dead in his tracks. His heart warmed and a smile crept across his face. *I have a daughter.* It was as if the realization had just swung down like a broadsword from the enemy's hand and hit him. If he was right, his daughter was as bonny as Abigale. Auburn hair, blue eyes, and a smile that could melt hearts. Aye, she had to be bonny.

Not able to contain himself any longer, James stopped an auld man walking by. "I have a daughter," he announced.

"Och, laddie, a wee one is a precious gift. One word of advice, keep her locked up and away from the lads." The man shook a finger at James. "They be rotten, I tell ye."

James smiled.

Excited beyond measure, he stopped another clan member. This time a woman. "Me daughter has been born." James grabbed the basket from her arms and walked with her to the washing station. He placed the basket down and hugged her as if she was his next of kin.

"Och, laird, if yer daughter be born, why are ye out here?" she asked.

He dinnae have an answer and could only hope Abigale would forgive him for being such an arse.

25

James's heart nearly shattered as he entered the crowded bedchamber and found Abigale pacing with their babe in her arms. It was obvious she had been crying.

He wanted to go to her and say what a fool he'd been, but the priest was on the way for the baptism.

Then he remembered, as laird he could do whatever he wanted! "Out! Everyone out!"

After the door shut, James strode over to his wife and daughter and wrapped his arms around them. "I'm sorry, lass, I was scared. Please forgive me." He held them tight. But Abigale didn't say a word.

"Say something, lass, or hit me."

Abigale's face was buried in his chest. "Love, I can no' breathe!"

James took a step back and gazed down at his wife to meet the most beautiful blue eyes.

"I knew ye would come back to me, but ye did give me a wee bit of a scare." She walked to the bed, sat on the edge of the mattress, and lovingly began to feed their daughter.

"James, we need a name for this wee one."

Witnessing such a beautiful thing, his beloved wife nursing their child, well, it made James feel an array of emotions inside. He trekked to the hearth to tend the fire, to work through his emotions. Things had changed drastically. Now he had two lives to protect—a wife and child, a family of his own.

"Do ye have a name in mind?" she asked.

"Nay." Damn him for being a fool.

Once the babe finished nursing, Abigale laced up the front of her shift. Lying the child down on a blanket, she swaddled her up, then held her to her chest until the wee one yawned and fell asleep.

"Ye are a wonderful mother," James said.

She smiled. "Do ye want to hold yer daughter?"

"I dinnae think I can. I will break her."

"Do no' be silly. Ye're her father, her protector," Abigale reassured him.

Carefully, James bent down and scooped the bundle up. She was so tiny and seemed to have disappeared into his hulking arms. Afraid of dropping her, James held her tight. She squirmed, and James watched as the corners of her tiny mouth turned down.

"No' so tight. Relax," Abigale said.

As he loosened his hold, Abigale smiled again as tears streamed down her cheeks.

James's brows creased in confusion. "Happy tears, aye?"

"Happy tears."

Abigale scooted over in the bed and motioned for him to come sit.

The bed gave a heavy moan as he sat next to his wife. He leaned back, resting the babe on his chest. His daughter took in a deep breath and let it out as she drifted to sleep again. She was an angel.

"See, she likes ye." Abigale peeked over his arm and caressed her daughter's cheek.

"Aye, I have that effect on the lassies," he jested.

Abigale chuckled.

James finally relaxed for the first time all day. "*Bele ange*, I tried to come to ye, to help ye, but..."

"Shh, I know." She kissed his arm and then laid her head on his shoulder. "I thought ye were mad at me."

"What? Abigale, why would ye think such a thing?"

Abigale soothed their daughter as she squirmed from the noise. "I was afraid ye were disappointed that we didnae have a son." Her shoulders drooped. "Ye must admit ye've been acting a wee bit strange."

"Abigale, I could no' be prouder of ye than I am right now. I was a wee bit nervous." James paused. "Shite, I will no' lie. I'm scared as hell."

"Me love, it's quite understandable to be scared. I am, too."

"Know this, Abigale. I love ye and I'm overjoyed to have a daughter. We will have a son—there's plenty of time." He winked at her.

Abigale snuggled next to her husband. "So, we need a name for our beautiful daughter."

At that moment, the babe cooed and gazed at her mothers. "James, look at her eyes. They're open. And so much like yers."

As he peered down at her, amber eyes stared back at him. He was speechless as a tear rolled down his cheek.

"I have the perfect name for her. Jaime," Abigale said.

"Jaime? Dinnae ye want to name her Bonnie?"

"Nay, just one look at her and everyone will know she's bonny. She looks just like her da. Just look at all that dark hair on her head." Abigale smoothed over a few strands of hair upon her daughter's head.

"Then Jaime it will be." James smiled and kissed wee Jaime on the forehead.

"I think it's time to let everyone in and do the baptism, aye?" Abigale asked.

"Aye." James moved off the bed, but Abigale grabbed his arm.

"Thank ye, James Douglas, for giving me Jaime and loving me."

"Och, lass I'll give ye many more." He kissed his wife thoroughly. "I love ye more than ye could ever know, my *belle ange*."

*A*s the baptism ceremony started, James and Abigale stood in front of the priest. The babe's godparents, Effie and Conall, stood next to them. Rory, Magnus, and Alice stood off to the side, watching happily.

The priest blessed Jamie, driving any evil from her body. James knew how important this was to Abigale, but for the life of him, he couldn't understand how evil could live inside an innocent babe. He'd protect his daughter from the darkness, nothing would ever hurt her.

After the blessing was over, Effie passed Abigale a white woolen gown with a small black and red embroidered dragon on it.

James admired the dragon and looked at Abigale. "'Tis for protection. Not only by her heavenly father but by her da," Abigale said.

James smiled and mouthed the words 'I love ye'.

~

*A*fter the ceremony, Conall watched everyone congratulate James and Abigale as he thought about his own happiness. There had been a time where he'd refused to forgive himself for the death of his wife and son. He hadn't deserved happiness, not while they had suffered a tremendous death. He'd never forget that. Nor would he forget that the elders had blessed him a second chance in life with another mate.

Effie showed him what it meant to be thoroughly loved. She'd almost sacrificed her own happiness to save him. That was true love.

As his gaze found Effie's from across the bedchamber, his body instantly warmed. Aye, the red-haired lass was his second chance, his redemption.

Effie joined him. "'Twas a beautiful ceremony, aye?"

"Aye," Conall pulled her close and wrapped his arms around her, placing his hands on her stomach. "I promise to be a good man to ye."

"Conall." Effie turned around. Confusion creased her brows. "Have I caused ye to think otherwise?"

"No—"

"Then stop right there." He felt the warmth of her hands as she cupped his face. "Ye're the most honorable man I know. I'm proud to be carrying yer babe and to be yer wife. Ye have made me dreams come true."

Conall smiled and gazed deeply into her green eyes. "I love ye."

"And I ye."

Conall claimed her lips, kissing her passionately.

Effie gasped and pulled away, placing her hands on her stomach. "Did ye feel it?"

"No."

"Here." Effie took his hands and placed them her stomach. "He's kicking."

Suddenly, he felt the tiniest kick. His eyes widened. That was his bairn. "A boy, aye?"

"I have a feeling." She shrugged. "He's strong just like his da."

A son? He was having a son.

26

"My lord, ye have a visitor."

Marcus, wrapped in a fur, looked up from the hearth. A visitor? Who would have tracked up this god-forsaken mountain and survived the blizzard?

Marcus glared at the man in black mail. "Well, who is it?"

Marcus was stronger after the Dragonkine female had healed him. His body was restored, his mind was sharp, but most of all, there were times he could feel the tiniest spark of his dragon. This gave him hope that maybe he could recover his beast.

"He would no' say, lord. Though he seems to be wounded and..." There was a long pause.

"Well...What?" His loud voice echoed in the cave, causing the Dragonkine female to cower as she huddled in the corner, hugging her knees to her chest.

"He's no' normal, deformed."

Wrapping the fur tighter around his shoulders, Marcus stood. "Well, bring him here."

"As ye wish, my lord."

Two men dragged the visitor in front of Marcus. Its body was limp and seemed to not be completely human. It had human legs, but the upper body left Marcus dumfounded.

The creature collapsed to its knees. As he raised his head, Marcus stepped back in disgust. The thing had two heads. Christ, one of its heads was dangling off its neck as if it had been broken.

Marcus examined the creature. The skin on its arms was covered in scales and its hands were talons. The damn thing stunk like a dung heap or more precisely, like walking death. Carefully, Marcus circled the beast, and the damn thing had a spiked tail like a dragon.

"What the hell are ye?" Marcus asked.

"I'm a wyvern." The creature coughed.

A two-headed wyvern? Marcus thought. He'd only seen one in his lifetime, for the creatures were rare and stayed secluded. They were much smaller than a dragon. However, this creature standing in front of him didn't resemble a wyvern. Two heads, and arms that hung to the ground. He looked closer at its arms and noticed a glimpse of a wing tucked against his body. *So, this is how it made it up the mountain, it flew.*

"Aye, I fought hard, lord, so hard." It rocked back and forth on its knees. "I fought to rule over Caerlaverock in the name of King Drest."

Marcus brows creased in confusion. "How do ye know about Drest?"

A slight moan escaped the mouth of its other half. Marcus stood in disbelief as it struggled to talk.

"Nay," the other half said. "Ye grew greedy. Ye wanted to rule for yerself."

"Shut up, ye fool," the creature hushed its wounded half. "Ye have no' say here."

The creature went back and forth, arguing with itself.

"Stop!" Marcus yelled. "It is apparent ye have gone mad." Marcus looked at one head and then to the other and corrected himself. "Ye two have gone mad. Why would I trust ye?"

Marcus had no time for the blubbering fool. "Take it away!" he ordered. "I have no use for a fool." Turning his back on the beast, Marcus walked back to where the Dragonkine female sat.

"My lord, I know who yer enemies be. Dragonkine, aye?"

Marcus stopped and turned to the creature.

"My lord, I can help ye fight the Kine."

Marcus rushed to the wyvern, angry it had dared speak to him again. "How do ye know about Dragonkine?" Cold breath puffed from Marcus's lips.

The creature trembled "One of them broke me neck, lord. I want me revenge just like ye want yers for what the Black Douglas did to ye."

"Ye didnae answer me question. Guards, off with its head... heads," Marcus ordered.

"Wait... wait." The wyvern struggled. "I know magic that can kill their dragons. Trust in me, my lord. Ye will have victory and revenge if ye allow me to live. Heal me, and ye shall see what I'm capable of," it pleaded.

Marcus didn't quite know what to do. Surely, he couldn't trust this vile beast. The creepers were his army, and when the time was right, he would unleash them into death dragons and destroy anyone who got in his way. He couldn't risk allying himself with a fool that could spoil his plan. Yet, a part of him, some dark and twisted part, wanted the Kine to suffer for expelling his dragon and banishing him from Scotland. Perhaps it would be useful after all.

"Who are ye?"

"Me name is Tavish Maxwell." The creature corrected himself, "Nay, my name is Tavish Black, my lord. I come to serve ye." He bowed his head.

EPILOGUE

Peering down on the village of Helmfirth, Marcus took in the land, planning his attack. Not an easy task, but one they'd follow through with in the name of King Drest.

Problem was, the laird of Helmfirth was established throughout Scotland for his barbaric battle tactics. His roots were planted deep in his clan's land and he would defend it to the death. He surrounded himself with bloodthirsty, battle ready warriors who fought for laird and land. Whoever dared to test his strength he laid waste to them. Even his own men who dared to get out of line. Mercy was something he never showed.

"Lord, they won't know what hit them." Tavish, now partly healed, sat on horseback next to Marcus. "I will personally gut the Red Hawk in yer honor."

Marcus hated to admit it, but he liked the creature's ruthlessness. Looking onto the village below, he watched a woman hang wet clothes on a drying line just outside her home. A group of men unloaded a cart full of freshly slaughtered meat into the butcher's shop. It looked to be a good payday for the man. Too bad they wouldn't live to spend it.

It had been a long time since he'd tasted blood. He gripped the hilt of his sword and licked his lips. Aye, the wee lambs were heading to slaughter and Helmfirth would be his.

"Aye, Tavish," Marcus concurred. "We'll attack the laird's weak spot, his people."

"Nay," the Dragonkine female, who was sitting behind Marcus, spoke up. "These are innocent people. Ye can no' kill them."

"I dinnae care." Marcus replied. "The true king will raise again and if that means a few innocent people die along the way, then that's the price they pay for choosing the wrong side."

"So ye're going to give them a choice?"

"Aye, join the dragon king or die." Marcus glanced at Tavish. The creature snickered in delight, apparently pleased at his new master's decision.

"Ye're pathetic." The Dragonkine female said.

"Pathetic?" Marcus dismounted and grabbed the female off the horse. "I think ye've became too comfortable around me. I didnae ask for yer opinion."

Marcus grabbed her arm and pulled her close to the cliff, making her look at the village. "Look, take it all in Female. These people mean nothing to me. They are humans. They slaughtered our king or have ye forgotten?"

The female shook her head. "I have no' forgotten, but where does it end. Ye can no' keep killing humans. We need them."

"My Lord," One of his guards interrupted. "Look." He pointed to the village.

Marcus grew still as he looked onto the village.

Everyone around him grew quiet as the he watched the town folk scurrying to move out of the way when a group of men on horseback approached the village square. The people bowed their heads as the men rode through.

The men were kilted and heavily armed with broadswords and battle axes. Their hair was long and messy, they were dirty; however, dominance shone heavy in their eyes. Their warhorses were just as intimidating, as they pawed at the earth waiting for the rest of the clansmen to catch up with them.

A hooded man on horseback rode straight up the middle of this spectacle, parting the sea of people even more. No one muttered a word, nor moved, as his dappled-gray horse stopped in front of his men. A goshawk as big as a buzzard was perched on his broad shoulder. Even though the hawk was unhooded, it rested without distress as its fierce red eyes searched the crowd.

The man removed his hood and revealed his identity. The town folk instantly bowed.

From atop his horse, the man looked as if he could reach the heavens. His appearance alone confirmed the rumors. Marcus couldn't get a good, detailed look at the man but the change in the air told him this was the Red Hawk of Helmfirth.

No one in the crowd would look the man in the eyes. Even from the high vantage point where Marcus sat, he could feel the man's power—his superiority.

Too bad such a fine specimen of a warrior would have to die. It seemed a waste of talent.

"My lord." A guard interrupted Marcus.

"Do we attack now?"

Looking at the size of Red Hawk's army, he needed to rethink his plan. His destiny was only a village away from the holy land and awaking his king. There was no time, nor excuses. He had to bring forth King Drest, but making a mistake would cost him so much.

"Nay. We make camp," Marcus said and turned to his horse. No one was going to stop him from making it to the holy land. He needed time to think, because right now he was in shock from the mere presence of what he had just seen; the Red Hawk of Helmfirth. In time he'd release the death dragon and there would be no saving Helmfirth.

PREVIEW OF BOOK 3 - HIGHLAND FATE

Chapter 1

Heavy footfalls thundered on the ground as Red Hawk strode through the village, infuriated. His broad shoulders twitched and his spine tingled as he immersed himself in thought. He palmed his sgian-dubh, throwing the damn thing up into the air and catching it by its hilt. *How could someone take his generosity for granted?*

The land of Helmfirth thrived with rolling fields of oats, properly equipped with healthy oxen to plow the earth. He'd made sure that the butcher in the village had a never-ending supply of the best meats and poultry and the finest equipment to do his job properly. In fact, Hawk had hunted game himself on several occasions in order to feed his people when times were hard.

There were men-at-arms who defended this land and fought for Hawk with vigor, putting their country before their own lives. And Helmfirth flourished.

In return all Hawk wanted was order in his village. The townsfolk had jobs to do and they did them well or suffered the consequences of disobedience. It was an eye-for-an-eye way of ruling over his people. It became personal when someone stole, cheated, or killed on his land. Not that it happened often, but when it did, he'd show no mercy. He was the Justiciar of Helmfirth, well respected and feared.

There was good reason why Red Hawk led with a tight fist. He didn't trust humans. Nay, he had learned long ago, when a human murdered his father, to keep his enemies close at hand. If it wasn't for his two sisters, he wouldn't give a rat's arse about these people. His sisters needed peace and to live normal human lives. He owed them that.

Undoubtedly the warrior protected this village with his life, making sure Helmfirth thrived for these people and this is how they repaid him? With thievery?

Hawk passed several townsfolk, never once sparing a glance at them. Every last one of them made his gut lurch. The folks knew better than to cross the brooding Highlander's path and scurried out of his way, bowing their heads so as not to meet his eyes.

As he heatedly treaded through the village, Hawk came across an auld woman who was selling fish. Because Helmfirth bordered the sea, it had a busy port for trade and was known for the freshest fish around. He sheathed his sgian-dubh and stopped in front of her. She was no stranger. Once, sometimes twice a day he would buy a bucket of fish from her, before making his way to visit his ferocious friends.

He threw the coins down on the table and snatched a pail. The woman knew better than to make small talk with the warrior today and nodded her head of graying hair, thanking him kindly for his purchase. Hawk humphed and strode off.

Reaching a small stone-fronted building with a thatch roof, he sharply came to a stop before he entered. He slammed the bucket down into the dirt and paced, resolving to calm the rage ripping through his body. This was his sanctuary and he needed to calm his backside down before he entered.

Taking a deep breath in through his nose, his jaw ticked and he exhaled. His dragon stirred relentlessly, begging to be released. His blood pulsed as he tamped down the urge to shift. Looking at the blue skies above him, the Highlander ran his fingers over his short red hair and composed himself, little by little. Once calm, he opened the door and with two strides he entered, bringing the bucket of fish with him.

Dust specks danced in the air as the sun shined through five of the windows lining the opposite wall. Feathers ruffled and talons pranced on perches as the raptors waited in their mews for their food. However, it wasn't entirely the provisions that made the birds of prey excitable; it was their master's presence.

One raptor in particular stood quietly as Hawk approached. The massive goshawk was unhooded and uncaged, perched alone on its jesses, showing remarkable patience as it waited for its master to prepare and tie a leather band around his forearm for the hawk to perch on.

It was illegal to own such prestigious animals, but Hawk cared naught. If caught the punishment was the severing of one's hands. Try as the mighty may, Hawk welcomed a confrontation with the sheriff or even the bloody king himself. If fact, slaying King Robert would right the wrong the king had done to his family years ago. Justice would finally be served.

Hawk worked his jaw back and forth as he tightened the leather strap. "Humans," he spat.

The quaint hut was nestled inside his forest out of sight of the village, and his birds were hidden well. Being the forest dragon he was, and because he spent so much of his time in the glen, he had rescued the five raptors from either starving, being abandoned or whatever other cruelty life had sprung on them. Even though he found great solace around all his birds, nothing came close to the bond he had with his goshawk, Arlen.

A shrill chirp softened his mood for the briefest moment as Hawk approached the raptor and motioned for it to perch on his arm. With ease and trust, the gray-spotted creature accepted and took its claim.

Making his way through the hut, he fed the rest of the birds of prey, marveling at their beauty. He paused and held out a fish to a petite falcon, a merlin. Beautiful and shaking, the female accepted the fish. Gently, Hawk lifted her wing and examined it. "Aye, lass, ye'll fly again." Holding the fish with her talons, the merlin fluffed her wing back against her body while she tore the flesh from the fish. She was the last of the five raptors to heal, and she was a beauty.

Hawk smiled and headed to the door, leaving the feathered beasts to eat.

Outside he looked to the blue crisp sky. It would be a perfect day, if it wasn't for the thief. He shook his head and strode over to a clearing in the glen. Arlen fluffed his feathers and squawked, waiting unwearied to take flight. Once Hawk gave the command the raptor spread its wings. With two pumps of his powerful wings he flew toward the clouds.

Hawk watched the goshawk as it commanded the blue arc and sliced through the clouds. He understood thoroughly how the bird felt in this moment, for he felt the same when he took to the sky, free and dominating.

Taking a seat next to a rowan tree, the warrior watched Arlen fly over the glen. Hawk didn't have as many years behind him as some of the other Dragonkine, nor had he been born dragon. He was of noble birth. His paternal grandmother was the sister of King John, the King of Scotland. His mother Johanna had ties to England; her grandmother had once been married to Edward I, King of England: two lines of royal descent, Gaelic and Norman. Aye, his life wasn't supposed to have turned out like this.

His father had been murdered by the King of Scotland himself, all in the name of the crown. This left his mother fleeing back to England where her heart had always been, leaving behind her three children.

Hawk blew out a frustrated breath as he thought about his mother. He was only a wee lad when she'd abandoned them. There were no goodbyes. As he recalled, the day she left the four of them were walking through the market square, Hawk holding his elder sister's hand and eating an apple while his little sister ran behind them, trying to catch up. From out of nowhere two men approached Johanna. Coin was exchanged and his mother turned and walked away from them, leaving her children with the men. Never looking back, she was gone and he had never seen her again.

The men were cruel as time went by. His sisters had become servants to the rogues, and Hawk was nothing more than a nuisance. Keeping him busy with stable duties kept him out of the stronghold and away from his sisters. Not the noble upbringing they were used to. One of the men, Liam, had quite the thirst for ale. When drunk, which was often, he would seek out Hawk and beat him for something the wee lad didn't understand. Never once had Hawk told his sisters about the abuse, and after a while he became numb to the beatings.

That was until the day Liam had taken it too far and left Hawk unconscious in the stables. Lana, his eldest sister, had found him bloodied and beaten, lying on soiled hay. Even after years passed the only remembrance he had of that night was that at evening meal, strangely, the two men fell asleep after Lana served them their ale. That dreadful night the three of them left the nightmare behind and were suddenly on their own.

Lana cared for Hawk and his younger sister, Gwen, just like a mother. After leaving the slave-house, she worked as a cook for a small clan and in return the abandoned children had a roof over their heads and food in their bellies. Lana had to grow up fast. There was no time to be a child.

When Hawk went through his transformation to Dragonkine, the siblings worked together to help him as he suffered through his muscles being ripped and his bones broken day after day until the change was completed. The girls hid him away from the clan when he was sick. Who knew what they would have thought, seeing such a sick wee lad? Surely they would have been accused of bringing the plague and doom upon the locals.

Indeed, Hawk would sell his soul in order to ensure his sisters' safety and well-being. He owed them that much. Hell, he owed the girls the world. So he took it upon himself to guarantee Lana and Gwen would never suffer again, although how he made that happen was his secret to keep, and the girls never asked how their brother came about owning Helmfirth.

Hawk leaned back against the rowan tree and rested his arms on his propped up knees as he watched his raptor soar down into the loch and catch a fish. Finally he relaxed as he pushed aside his childhood thoughts. He had bigger issues at hand. Someone had stolen from him and the fool had to pay for such a crime.

Leaving his second-in-command, Brodie MacGregor, to deal with the thief had been a tough call, but it had to be done, for Hawk was too angered. And when he was this angry he had a difficult time keeping his dragon stilled. He felt the change overcoming his body. He felt the compulsion to shift.

Lana and Gwen were the only ones who knew his secret and he wanted to keep it that way. Surely some of his men-at-arms had their suspicions, but no one dared to speculate or spread rumors. Hawk kept the village safe, which outweighed any ramblings about a dragon.

If he had his way he would shift into dragon permanently, and live in the glen far away from the townsfolk. Life would be much simpler as a dragon.

Crunching leaves coming from behind him startled Hawk and he jumped to attention, ready to attack.

"Shite, MacGregor, ye must no' sneak up on me like that!"

MacGregor approached with his hands held up in surrender. "My laird." He bowed his head. "I thought ye knew to expect me. The thief has been placed in the pillory and awaits his punishment."

Every bit of pent-up irritation coursed within his veins, pumping rage all over his body. Hawk felt his dragon gain control and his spine stiffen. Ruby-red waves rippled across his eyes. It was time the thief paid.

MacGregor looked to the ground and stood silent while he waited for the Hawk's command.

Cracking his neck from side to side and rolling his massive shoulders back and forth, Hawk made his way back to the village. He held out his right arm and within seconds Arlen landed on his forearm. The bird fluffed his feathers and settled in.

"Och, what did the fool have to say?" Hawk asked as the two men walked toward the village square.

"Nothin'. In fact he hasn't said a word."

"Beg for mercy?" Hawk gave MacGregor a sideways glance.

MacGregor took a double look at Hawk's eyes. They were normal again. "Nay." He paused. "I think the fool may be daft."

Strictly true. Anyone in their right mind would never attempt to steal from the Red Hawk. He cared naught that the stolen property was a stale loaf of bread. Thievery was thievery. Someone had worked hard to bake that bread, had paid for it. And then to cause a ruckus and claim the sweet auld lady had lied and accused the wrong man... Well, that was absurd.

Hawk and MacGregor approached the village with purpose as the last rays of sunlight were settling into dusk. One thing was certain; if this fool made him late to the evening meal he would have the eejit's head. Being late to any meal was inexcusable and furthermore, disrespectful.

As the men strode farther into the town square, a throng of townsfolk gathered around the pillory. The crowd separated as Hawk walked past; MacGregor followed closely behind. Two of his men-at-arms who were standing guard, bowed their heads at Hawk.

"This is the fool?" Hawk eyed the warriors sternly.

"Aye."

He observed the man. His head and his hands were trapped between two pieces of wood, hollowed out so his neck and wrists had little room to move. The man was forced to stand while his head was face down so he could only see the ground. *Pathetic,* Hawk thought.

The Highlander towered over the thief as he perched the goshawk on the pillory. The bird shrieked out loud and pecked the man's ear, causing him to cry out in pain.

"Ye dinnae belong here, do ye?" Hawk crossed his arms over his chest.

"And what makes ye think that?" the thief asked as he wrinkled his face in pain.

As if the goshawk knew that the man was disrespecting his master, he pecked at the man's cheek, breaking the skin.

"One thing ye should know is that I ask the questions. Ye have no rights here!" Hawk's voice, low and deep, carried across the square. The crowd shuddered and mothers grabbed their children close.

Hawk strode toward the back of the pillory. "Everyone here knows ye no' steal from me, unless ye have a death wish."

A sinister laugh slowly escaped the thief.

In one fluid motion Hawk was in front of him. He lifted his knee and bashed the man in the mouth. "Ye mock me? Are ye senseless?"

The thief spat blood and tried to lift his head. "Och, ye see, ye all be already dead."

Hawk grabbed a handful of the man's hair and yanked it back until the wood dug into his neck. "What do ye mean, we are all dead?"

The thief struggled to talk. "Why...should I tell ye? All I wanted was to fill me belly."

Thievery was now the last thing on Hawk's mind. How was he supposed to protect his sisters and his village if he didn't know what this fool was conjuring?

"Thief," Hawk lowered his head to ear level so the fool could hear him loud and well, "I know ye be a stranger and ye dinnae belong here, which leads me to believe ye came with ill intentions. Ye can make this easier on yerself and tell me what's coming, or I can beat it out of ye."

The man gave Hawk a twisted smile. At this point Hawk was left with no other choice. One way or another he would get the information he wanted. He nodded and the goshawk charged the man's head, pecking out his eye. The thief screamed out in agonizing pain.

"Are ye ready to talk?" Hawk asked. "Or shall Arlen take yer other eye?"

"Aye!" The man was breathless. "Please!"

For Hawk, patience had never been a virtue and this fool had pushed him to the limit. "Go on then."

Blood dripped from the stranger's right eye and his voice shook. "Ships will be entering the harbor in less than a day's time."

"Ships? And who is advancing this attack on Helmfirth?" As peaceful as Hawk tried to be, there was always someone out there craving what was his. Or someone wanting to challenge him. But who? Helmfirth was secluded, with not a neighboring clan around for at least a three-day ride.

"It's no' who, my laird, it's death."

"How am I supposed to trust ye?" Hawk demanded.

"Och my laird, that's a risk ye must be willing to take."

"Bastard!" Hawk shoved the man's head away and paced in front of the pillory. What was he going to do? *I can no' trust this eejit. But what if he's right and Helmfirth is in danger?* If he could spew his venomous poison right now and melt the skin from this fool's body, he would do it quicker than he could shift.

MacGregor came up behind him and stood shoulder to shoulder. "My laird, I can lead half of our men to the harbor while the other half stay here to protect the village."

Always prepared and ready for battle, it was like MacGregor to have a plan. It was one of the reasons Hawk trusted him and had allowed him to wed Lana. He was an honorable man who provided for his family and fought for Helmfirth.

"Nay, send full force. I'll stay here tonight and meet ye on the morrow."

"Aye." MacGregor strode toward the stables, motioning his men to follow suit.

Hawk sent the thief a vile stare as he quit the square, calling over his shoulder to one of the guards, "And chain this thief in the dungeon. I'm no' done with him yet."

Without hesitation two of his men busied themselves obeying their laird's command.

No doubt one dragon, especially with his size and deadly venom, could protect Helmfirth if the threat showed true. He wasn't scared of death; in fact he welcomed it, dared it. There was a reason his stronghold had held throughout the years: magic. No amount of weapons or strategic war tactics could penetrate the power of magic. As long as he lived, which was forever, this village would be protected. His sisters would be safe, but he had to keep his head.

Hawk's belly rumbled as soon as he opened the doors to the great hall. The aroma of cooked fish, vegetables, and bread made his mouth water. The cooks had done a fine job this eve. The hall at Helmfirth was only half filled as the Red Hawk's warriors prepared for battle and their journey to the harbor. Still the thief had left him unsettled, which irritated him. All he wanted to do was enjoy his meal with a peaceful mind.

Hawk sat his big body down at a table in front of a trencher and started to pile the night's provisions high. The scowl on his face was more than a warning that he wanted to be left alone.

"Ye dinnae have to be a grump all the time," Lana said as she sat across from her brother and filled a tankard with mead.

Hawk glanced up, chewing a mouthful of bread. "Lana." He swallowed. "I do no' need yer teasing."

Lana handed the tankard to him. "I know, but if ye smile once in a while, ye might grab the attention of a lass. Ye have a handsome smile, Hawk."

"I need no lass. Ye and yer sister keep me busy enough." He took a long pull from the tankard. "Just the other day I had to get rid of a lad pursuing Gwen's womanly virtues."

"Och, brother, please tell me it wasn't the Drummond lad," Lana said disappointedly.

"Aye! I picked the lad up by the seat of his trews and kicked his arse oot. That one is no good, Lana. Trust me, I know."

Gwen's beauty caught the attention of many lads. Keeping that lass's virginity intact until she wed was going to be the death of him.

Lana shook her head and filled her trencher. "I guess that makes me lucky. Ye liked MacGregor." She smiled as her husband's name passed her lips.

Hawk looked at his sister and grumbled, shoving a piece of fish in his mouth.

At that moment MacGregor appeared in the great hall, making his way to his wife as he balanced one of his sons on his shoulders and one wrapped around his leg while the eldest lad walked proudly beside him. "There be me bonny wife." He bent down and kissed Lana on the cheek.

"Good eve, husband. Are ye hungry?" Before MacGregor could answer, the three mischievous lads called out in unison, "Meeee!" Lana giggled and grabbed three trenchers, filling them with food.

Hawk peered up to watch the chaotic feeding frenzy and smirked. Lana was happy and had a loving family, a family she deserved. Then he looked at MacGregor, who had caught him smiling. MacGregor smiled back. "Ye know life is worth living when the right lass comes along."

Hawk's moment of good spirits turned serious and tiresome. Why the sudden interest in his love affairs? It was not that he didn't enjoy a lass; he had never tried it.

Settling down, taking a wife was not a topic he visited much. This was a touchy subject for most Dragonkine, though deep down he had thought about how it would feel to be loved by a lass. He had dared to think about waking up in the morn next to a soft warm female body. But Hawk was smart; he protected his heart and would never allow himself to chase that dream. It would only bring him heartache and despair and, frankly, he'd had enough of that in his life. An immortal dragon life did have its downfalls.

The warrior stiffened his spine and acted as if he hadn't heard MacGregor's comment. "Are your men ready for travel?"

"Aye. I wanted to kiss me wife farewell before I left. We'll ride through the night and arrive at the harbor before sunrise."

"Good." Hawk drank from his tankard of ale.

"My laird, are ye sure ye want all of our men at the port? We can spare a few to stay behind."

"Do ye query me command?" Hawk peered at him sternly.

"Nay, my laird."

"Good. Now if ye will excuse me, I'm going to me bedchamber." He took a loaf of bread with him as he stood, but before he left the great hall he said his farewells to Lana and kissed her boys on the top of their heads.

"Uncle Hawk," the eldest boy called out. "When can ye and da take me huntin'?"

"Och, I dinnae…"

"I've been practicing wit' me bow real good. Haven't I Da?" The boy gleamed at his father excitedly.

MacGregor smiled proudly. "Aye, ye have, but yer uncle is a verra busy man. When I return I'll take ye huntin'."

The boy's look of disappointment crushed Hawk like a boulder slamming into him. He never allowed himself to get close to the boys, or MacGregor, as a matter of fact. It was easier on him to stay away and be alone. It had taken a long time to build up these walls; he wasn't going to let them be breached by anyone.

Hawk could no longer look at his nephew without feeling like an arse, so he strode off to his bedchamber, once again alone.

To continue Hawk and Kate's story, pick up a copy of Highland Fate, Guardians of Scotland Book 3:

Preview of Book 3 - Highland Fate

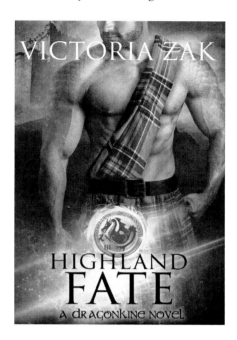

About Victoria Zak

Victoria Zak is an internationally bestselling author of historical and contemporary romance. She weaves magic into her timeless tales, reminding readers anything is possible, especially with a dragon by your side. Raised in Dunedin, Florida, the sister city to Stirling, Scotland, no wonder she grew up fascinated with anything Scottish. Add the ocean into the mix, and it's easy to see where Victoria found inspiration for her stories.

As a child, she read anything she could get her hands on, which developed into full-scale book addiction by adulthood. Curious by nature, Victoria doesn't shy away from anything. She enjoys historical research and hanging out at the nearest coffee shop. Victoria currently resides in Maryland with her real-life heroes, her husband and two children.

Victoria loves to hear from her readers. You can connect with her through the links below:

www.victoriazakromance.com
victoria@victoriazakromance.com
Newsletter http://bit.ly/1uebjmR

facebook.com/VictoriaZakAuthor

bookbub.com/authors/victoria-zak

instagram.com/victoriazakromance

twitter.com/VictoriaZak2

BOOKS BY VICTORIA ZAK

Guardians of Scotland Series:

Highland Burn

Highland Storm

Highland Fate

Highland Destiny

Highland Hope

Ember Brooke Series:

Scorched Hearts

Hearts Under Fire

Daughters of Highland Darkness Series:

Beautiful Darkness

Deadly Darkness

Wicked Darkness

Hell's Cowboys Series:

My Immortal Cowboy

Stand Alones:

Once Upon a Winter Solstice

The Jewel of Grim Fortress

Midnight's Kiss

Manufactured by Amazon.ca
Acheson, AB